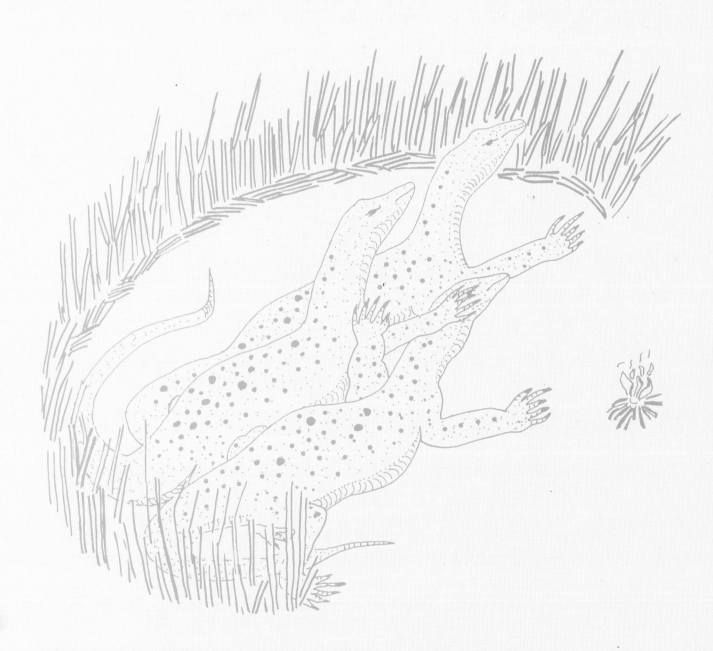

Tjarany

Tjaranykura Tjukurrpa ngaanpa kalkinpa wangka tjukurrtjanu

Gracie Greene

Joe Tramacchi

Lucille Gill

Magabala Books

Roughtail

The Dreaming of the Roughtail Lizard
and other stories told by the Kukatja

Gracie Greene

Joe Tramacchi

Lucille Gill

Magabala Books

Acknowledgements

We wish to thank members of the Wirrumanu (Balgo), Malarn (Mulan, Lake Gregory) and Yaka Yaka (Yagga Yagga) communities for their support and permission to publish these stories. The authors would like to acknowledge the traditional source, language and ownership of the stories, some of which belong to other tribal groups too. Thanks to Sundown Ellery, Mary Djaru, Patsy Mudgadell, Christine Mudgadell, Helen Nagamara, Pauline Sunfly, Donald Matthews and to Matthew Wrigley of Kimberley Language Resource Centre who, with Vonnie Brown of Luurnpa School at Wirrumanu, systematised the written Kukatja. Thanks also to Merrilee Lands, Carol Tang Wei, Kim Ackerman, Warwick Nieass, Kerry Davies, Taz Garstone, Phillip Woodhill, Ken Nielson, Joe Edgar and Goolarabooloo Arts and Crafts, Broome.

First published 1992
Revised and reprinted 1993
Published in paperback 1996
Reprinted 1999
by Magabala Books Aboriginal Corporation, 2/28 Saville Street, PO Box 668, Broome WA 6725
email: magabala@tpgi.com.au

Magabala Books receives financial assistance from the Commonwealth Government through the Australia Council, its arts funding and advisory body, and the Aboriginal and Torres Strait Islander Commission. The State of Western Australia has made an investment in this project through ArtsWA in association with the Lotteries Commission.

Editor Peter Bibby
Designer Narelle Jones
Design Consultant Sava Pinney
Production Coordinator Donna-Marie Ifould
Production Consultant Simon MacDonald

Photography Brian Stevenson, Perth
Printed by Tien Wah Press (Pte) Ltd, Singapore
Typeset in Souvenir

National Library of Australia
Cataloguing-in-Publication data

Greene, Gracie, 1949- .
Tjarany roughtail: the dreaming of the roughtail lizard and other stories told by the
Kukatja = Tjarany: tjaranykura tjukurrpa ngaanpa kalkinpa wangka tjukurrtjanu.

Includes index

ISBN 1 875641 30 0

1. Kukatja (Australian people) - Legends. 2. Legends - Australia
- Kimberley (WA). 3. Kukatja language - Texts - Juvenile literature.
4. Aborigines, Australian - Western Australia - Kimberley - Legends.
I. Tramacchi, Joe, 1954- . II. Gill, Lucille, 1956- . III. Title.

398.20899915

Cover painting (detail) by Lucille Gill.

Western Australia

artswa

Australia Council for the Arts

These are our stories.
We give permission for Gracie and Lucy and Joe
to tell them, so you can share them.
We hope you enjoy Roughtail.

Kukatja people
of Malarn, Yaka Yaka
and Wirrumanu communities

*Kimberley Aboriginal Law and Culture A.G.M.
Mt Barnett, October 1989*

Kutjuwarra Wangka

Contents

When you hear this word . . .

… it's a good one. Little word. When they see this book, good, small word. Might be a good one when you see it. From everywhere people can have a good look. When they see this book, big mob of stories, you've got a lot of stories. Now you've got to listen to my stories. Good. Little word. Maybe you might think it's good. Little word.

Many people told these stories, not just me. They put together plenty of words, a lot of stories. You'll see them! One word, one language. You've got to hear this. Maybe you won't see it, this good word. You can't look around for any more words. Good words. These words will stand up. People will see them. That's what I'm saying. This small word.

Sundown Ellery

Do you like this word? Is it good? Maybe it's no good! Will many other people like these Aboriginal stories, these stories in the language of our people?

We're talking just like you. Do you understand? Is it good? We speak Kukatja, you speak English. Do you like our language? We're talking among ourselves, person to person. In our way, people sit down and listen to each other's word in turn, like you do.

Do you like the way we tell our stories? Well that's all, no more.

Will I say some more words?

In our camps and around our homes and their homes, they might like this book and read it or maybe they won't. They might say this is all no good or they might like it. Maybe this book won't be used in schools.

Where did this language come from? From Balgo or Malarn, a big mob of people speak this language. Wangkatjungka is ours. Kukatja. You've got your own language. It's good, and so is mine. These two languages together. We listen to your language. Grown ups and children can understand what kartiya say when they're talking to them. No more.

Mary Djaru

This was first spoken and recorded in Kukatja, and then translated, by Mary and Sundown.

The stories were told by Gracie in Kukatja and English, while she was visiting Lucy and Joe at Noonkanbah, about halfway between Wirrumanu (Balgo) and Broome, in Christmas 1987. Helen Nagamara, Patsy Mudgadell and Christine Mudgadell wrote the stories out in Kuktatja. Joe Tramacchi wrote them in English.

Kartiya means a non-Aboriginal person. Mary's surname is pronounced Tjartju.

The Kukatja word Tjukurrpa is written in English as Dreaming, the word Tjukurrta as Dreamtime, to follow the usage of the storyteller. Both of these words convey an idea of creative time which draws together the distant past and the living present. As Gracie Greene says: "All this is still here today."

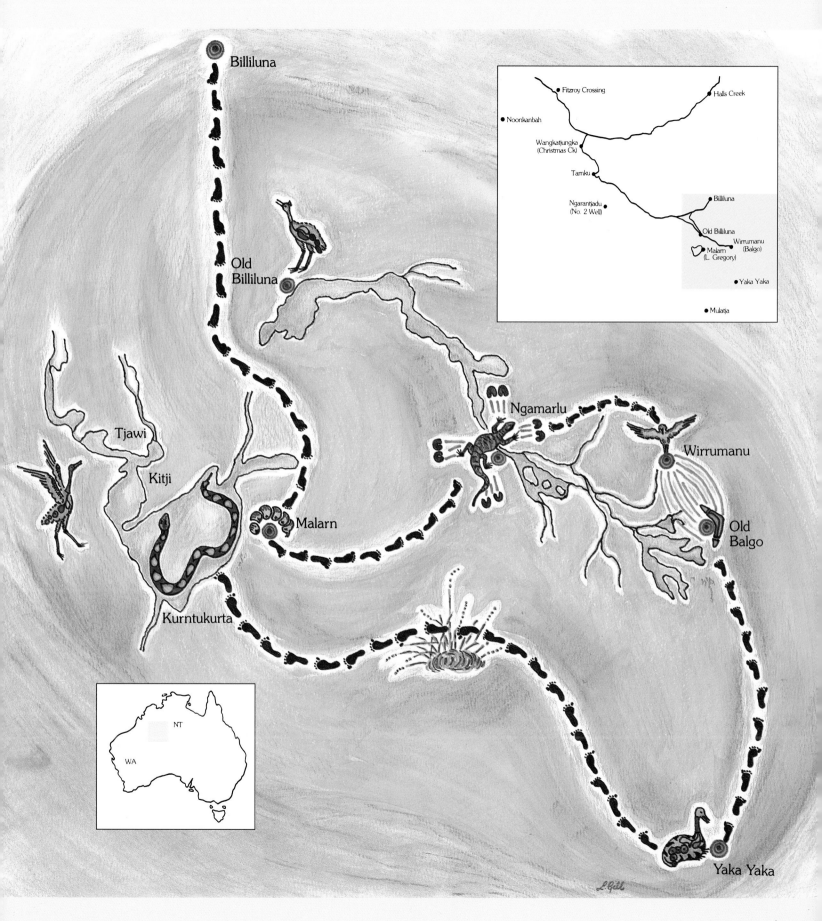

Billiluna

Old
Billiluna

Ngamarlu

Wirrumanu

Old
Balgo

Tjawi

Kitji

Malarn

Kurntukurta

Yaka Yaka

Fitzroy Crossing

Halls Creek

Noonkanbah

Wangkatjungka
(Christmas Ck)

Tarnku

Ngarantjadu
(No. 2 Well)

Billiluna

Old Billiluna

Wirrumanu
(Balgo)

Malarn
(L. Gregory)

Yaka Yaka

Mulatja

NT

WA

L Gill

1

The Roughtail Lizard Dreaming

A long time ago in the Dreamtime,
there lived a Roughtail Lizard man
who had a lot of Dreaming
and songs he kept to himself.
One day he was sitting by a waterhole
called Ngamarlu, when some men,
who were staying by the water,
heard him singing.

Night after night those men got up to
listen to that Roughtail man singing his
songs as he sat by the fire. Every day
when the men passed his camp they
heard his singing. All the old people
came together and they sat around,
talking among themselves. They
decided to send someone to meet him.
"Go and ask that Roughtail man to
sing us a song," they said. That person
went over and asked him, "Show us
how to sing one of your songs."

Tjaranykura Tjukurrpa

Kurralka Tjukurrtja Tjaranypa nyinama
kutju kalyungka, Ngamarlungka.
Puntuya tjiingka kalyungka nyinama,
kulinuya turlku yinkarra nyinama tjiilu
Tjaranytju. Mungakutjupa
mungakutjupangka pakaraya kulinma.
Tjarany tjiitja warungkama nyinama
turlku yinkarraka.

Nyinanguya yungunkutjupangka,
tjapirnungkuya, "Yarralalu
tjapila tjiingka Tjaranytja
turlkulampa yinkawa.
Turlku palyaminyirri
yinkalkuwa."
Pakarnuya
kutjungkarringu
yirna-yirna. Yanuluya
tjapirnu, "Tjaranytja
turlkulanyatju
kutju nintitjurra?"

Rockhole

Roughtail Lizard

Men

The Roughtail man answered,
"Certainly! I'll give you my songs
to learn." Then he called them
all together and made them sit
down and he gave to each man
a song. He was putting white
ochre on their chests, and
saying to them, "I'll give you
this white ochre to put on
your chests. All these songs
are to be sung with ochre."

"Yuwu!
Nintitjunkurnanyurranya
tjiitja yungku ngayukurnu."
Manutjananya nyinatjunu
puntu kutjuwarra turlkukurlu.
Tjunamatjananya
mawuntu ngarrkawana.
Watjarnmatjana,
"Ngaatjananta
tjunku mawuntu
ngarrkawana."

3

One by one he gave each
man a different song. Over
and over he put the white
ochre on them, telling them,
"This day I'm giving all these
songs to the men. When I
put this stuff on your chests,
you may start to sing."

Then he began singing for
them and as he sang
he showed them dances.
When he had finished
he said, "I give these songs
to the men to keep, each
one in his own camp,
a different song for each."

And so from north to south,
from east to west, each has his song
from the Dreamtime. Today if you
go over there to Wirrumanu
you can see this waterhole called Ngamarlu.

Tjiikura turlkuku kutjun-kutjunpa.
Tjunamatjananya mawuntu nayakarralu.
Parratjananya watjarnma,
"Ngaanpa kuwarrirnanyurranya
tjuninpa puntungka. Turlku kanyirnin
ngaantu laltulu mawuntulu.
Katjinanyurranya tjunku ngarrkangka
tjiitjanyurra turlku yinkalku."

Tjiitjanu turlkutjanampa
yinkarnma. Yinkarnu
nintitjunutjananya
wiyarnukatjitjanampa
watjarnu, "Puntululpinyurra
ngaatja turlku kanyila
ngurra kutjupangurra
kutjupatjanulu."

Kakarralu, yurlpayirralu, kayililu,
wiluralu turlkuya tjiitja manu
tjukurrpa. Kuwarri katjin yanku
kakarra Wirrumanukutu. Yankun
nyaku tjiitja kalyu Ngamarlu.

*Here are some of the stories that people have sung
and danced since that time.*

Wirrumanu is also called Balgo

4

The Crow and the Eagle

How the crow came to be black.

Long ago in the Dreamtime,
the crow was white. The crow
and the eagle were the best of friends.
They lived together in
the same camp. When they
got up in the morning,
the crow used to tell the eagle,
"You go up into the hills and
look for the big red hill kangaroo.
I will go down to the billabong
and see if I can catch some
ducks for our dinner."

The eagle went up into the hills
and the crow went down to the billabong
and caught lots of ducks!
He had a hairstring tied around his
waist and he used a long, hollow reed
to breathe underwater.
He'd jump into the water
and sink below the surface.
When the ducks were passing,
he would grab them by the legs,
one by one, and tuck
them in the hairstring
around his waist.

When he had enough,
he'd get out of the water
and make a big fire
and start cooking the ducks.
Every day he had a good feed there,
then he would go back to camp
empty-handed.

Kaarnka Kamu Kurnkangalku

Nyaalpakarralu kaarnka marurringu.

Tjukurrtapula kurralka nyinama
Kaarnka kamu Kurnkangalku
nyinamapula palya. Ngurrangka
kutjungkapula nyinama, katjipula
pakarnma Kaarnkalura watjala,
"Kurnkangalkulu nyuntun yarra
kankarra pamarrkutu parraran nyawa
tjarluku marluku pamarrkarratjaku."
Kaarnkalura watjarnu, "Ngayurna
mayankurna kaninytjarra kilikiwana
nyakunara tjaalalypaku.
Mankuwarna mirrkaku tjiitja."

Kurnkangalku yanu kankarra
pamarrwana, tjiitja Kaarnka yanu
kaninytjarra kilikiwana yanu manama
tjaalalypa laltu. Palurulu kanyirnu
tunkulpakarrpirnungku nyirntjiwana
tjiitjanulu. Palunyalu manu wurkarlpa
tawarra yarlakulu. Paluru kaninytjarra
wirlutingu kalyungka nyinama
yirlanmatjananya tjaalalypa
kaninytjarra kalyungurulu. Katjiya
wayintanama kankarrawanalu
palunyalutjananya ngaluratjunama
katjiya mirri nyinama.

Katjiraya lalturringu pakarnu yanu
ngarama kankarra yitiwana waru tjarlu
tilirnu paarnutjananya ngalangu
tjaalalypa. Nayakarra paluru tjilanyarrima
yungunkutjupa-yungunkutjupa tjilanyalu
ngalkura wiyanma ka yanama ngurrakutu
marumpu kutjarra. Wiyatji marlaku
yanama ngurrakutu.

5

Every day the eagle came home and asked the crow, "Have you any tucker for me?" And the crow would say, "Sorry, I didn't catch anything today." He always told the eagle to go up into the hills to look for kangaroo. Then one day the eagle thought, "That crow is up to something! He's telling me lies."

So he came back earlier than usual but he didn't go to the camp. No, he went to the billabong to catch the crow at his tricks. He saw the crow rushing around hiding the cooked ducks under some leaves.

Nayakarra marlaku yanama Kurnkangalku ngurrakutu tjapila Kaarnka, "Kurlun kanyirnin mayi ngayuku?" Kaarnkalura watjala, "Yuwayi wiyarnungkura."

"Wiyarna purtu parra ngalula wiya minyirri wiyarna ngalku kuka pankarrpari." Nayakarralu mayitjurra tjiingka Kurnkangalkungka. Tirrutjurralu nayakarralu pakara mayitjunama, "Nyuntun yarra kankarra marlukuran pamarrkutu." Tjiilu Kurnkangalkulu kulinma, "Mayitjuninparni!" Kurnkangalkulu watjarnu, "Mayitjuninparni!" Wulu kulinma tjiilu Kurnkangalkulu.

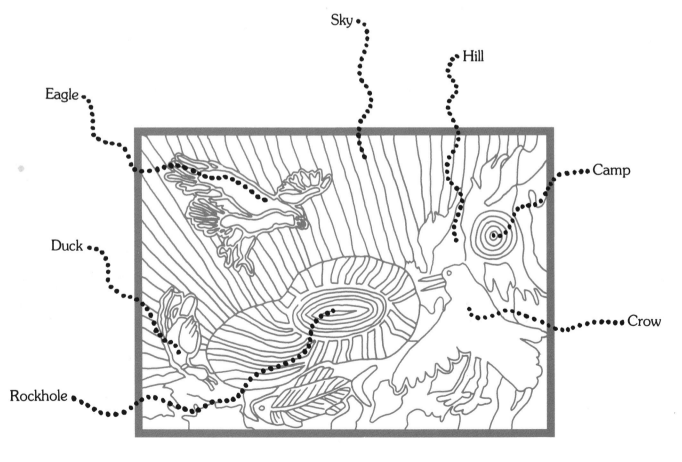

When he came near, the eagle asked the crow, "Have you kept any food for me?" The eagle started rushing about, looking here and there as if he was trying to find something.

Then eagle saw some grease on the hot ashes and around the crow's mouth, where he'd been eating, and there was grease on the crow's hands. "This fire has grease on it!" shouted the eagle. "So that's what you've been up to. You've been hiding my share of the food, and telling me lies!"

Tjiitja Kaarnka yanu kaninytjarra kilikikutu, yanu tjaalalypa pungkura, ngalkunma warungka. Tjiilu Kaarnkalu nyangu Kurnkangalku yanulu parra wirrtjanma parra yakatjunama tjiitja tjaalalypa tjalyirrwana karratalu.

Tjiitjana Kurnkangalkulu tjapirnu, "Kuka wayin kanyirnin? Wiyalka ngaatja waru tjira wiyatju? Yakatjunamatjuran ngalkuma kuka ngayuku nganakurnin mayitjunama!"

7

Eagle got very angry, grabbed the crow
and threw him into the hot ashes.
The crow jumped out of the fire
but the eagle kept on throwing him
back onto the coals, until he was
burnt black all over.

Some of the eagle's feathers were burnt
too. That's why he's brown. The crow
was punished for his greediness
and that's why he's black today.

Tjiitjanu Kurnkangalkulu
manu tupurltjunu
warungka
witulu kutjupa
tuwurntjunu katji
marurringu.

Palunyangka
kawurnwana tjiitja
Kurnkangalku parra
punkanma.

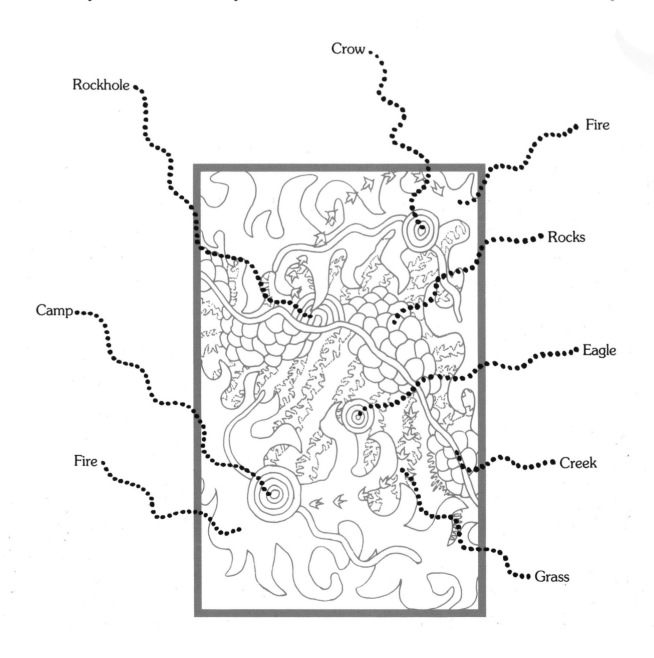

The Emu and the Turkey

This story started somewhere east of Yaka Yaka.
(We say that as Yagga Yagga. It means Quiet Quiet.)

Long time ago, turkey
and emu were the best of friends.
They used to go hunting together.
One day the turkey and
the emu both had children.
The emu had a lot of chicks
and the turkey had two.

The emu came up to turkey and took
her to see all the emu chicks.
After that the emu saw the turkey's
two children. They were very pretty,
lovely little chicks. Then the turkey
went back to her camp.

Karlaya Kamu Kiparapula

Ngaatja Tjukurrpa Yaka Yaka Kakarra.

Kurralka Tjukurrta, Kipara kamu
Karlayapula nyinama, yarrapula
wartilpa lurrtjukirli. Tjirntungka
kutjungka Kipara kamulupulanyaya
Karlayalu tjiitji kanyirnma. Karlayalu tjiitji
laltu kanyirnma. Kiparalupulanya
kutjarra kanyirnma.

Karlayalu yanu nyangu Kipara
nyawatjutjana tjiitji, Karlayalupulanya
nyangu Kiparalulkapulanya tjiitji kutjarra
kanyirninpa. Palya minyirripula
mikuputarri. Kiparanga wurna
yanu ngurrakutu.

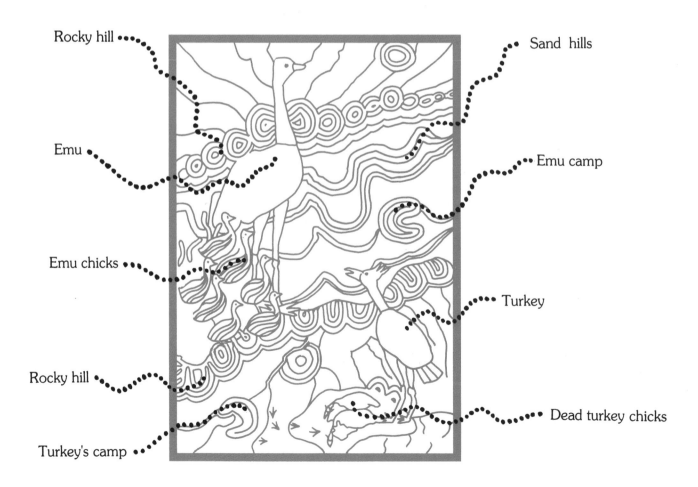

Rocky hill

Sand hills

Emu

Emu camp

Emu chicks

Turkey

Rocky hill

Turkey's camp

Dead turkey chicks

10

The emu was so jealous that she thought
up a plan to get rid of the turkey's chicks.
Then she called out to her own
chicks. The mother emu told
all her chicks to hide
in a big clump of spinifex grass.

When the emu chicks were hiding,
the emu went over to turkey's camp
and said to her, "I killed all my children!"
The turkey was very shocked. "Why did
you do that?" she asked. "Because I don't
like having chicks around me," emu told
turkey. "It's too much trouble for me
getting feed for them and looking after
them all the time." Then emu said
to the turkey, "Why don't you
kill your two little ones?"

Then the emu went away to her camp.
She was peeping from her camp, watching
to see if the turkey would kill her two little
ones. The turkey hit them on the neck
with a nulla nulla and the two little chicks
were dead.

Emu got up when she saw what
had happened. She quickly called
out to her chicks. They all came
running to her from their hiding place.

Then turkey saw what the emu had done.
Turkey got the big nulla nulla and hit
herself on the head, crying for her twins,
sitting on the ground throwing sand
all over herself. All that day
the turkey was crying,
mourning for her two little chicks.

Karlayalu kulinma,
"Nyaalpankurnapulanya
ngaakutjarra?" Yarltingupulampa,
"Yanamarniyawu!" Karlayalu
watjarnu, "Yarraya
yakayarra marnkalta."

Katjiya yakayanu
Karlayalura yanu
Kiparakurnu ngurrakutu.
Watjarnulu Kiparalu,
"Wiyarnatjananyaya
ngayulu tjiitji kanyirninpa.
Ngayulurnatjana
tjiitji pungu,"
watjarnulu Karlayalu.
"Puwapulanya tjiikutjarralpi!"
watjarnu Karlayalu.

Karlayangkura yanu
ngurrakutu. Nyangamara
yakalu Ngurratjanulu.
Pungupulanya
nyankawana kuturukurlu
kapula mirringu.

Karlayalupulanya pakarnu
nyangu. Walytjakutjanampa
yarltingu tjiitjiku,
"Yanamarniyawu!" Ngalyalpiya
taputjunama wurrkaltjanu.

Nyangulu Kiparalu Karlayangka.
Manu kuturu Kiparalukangku
yatunma kata yulakarralu
tjiitji kutjarraku. Wirrupungulpi
pamarrpanga. Kiparangkura
wulu yulama.

12

Early next morning she got up and went
out bush, up into the sand hills. She took
with her a coolamon and a digging stick.
She came to where all the kumpupatja,
the bush tomatoes, grow.
She started picking them.

When the turkey had filled her coolamon
up, she sat down, cleaned out the fruit
and separated the seeds.
She put the seeds in the coolamon.
Those seeds were very hot, like chilli,
burning hot. Then when she'd done that,
turkey went back home to her camp.

She waited until the emu went to sleep.
She went over with her coolaman full
of seeds. She went up close to the emu,
and started putting seeds on both her
eyes, until the emu's eyes were covered.
The turkey went back to her camp
and waited. She was watching,
waiting for the emu to wake up.

The emu woke up and stretched.
Then she rubbed her eyes. While she
was rubbing her eyes the seeds started
burning her. She got a very big fright.
She jumped up, crying, bouncing up
and down on the ground. She was
crying for three days in her camp.

Pakarnu yanu
taliwana manu
luwanytja kamu wana.
Yanutjananya
manama
kumpupatja.

Katjiraya lalturringu
yanu nyinatingutjananya
pirrinma kumpupatja.
Yanu marlaku ngurrakutu.
Katji kutunngarringu
Karlaya, yanulu kinti
nyinama Karlayangka.

Tjunulu
paniyangka
kumpupatja
katjirra
kampangu
paniya.
Yanu yakalu
nyangama.

Karlayangkura
pakarnu
yunguntjarrakangku
pirrinmangku paniya.
Ngurlungkura yulama
kamu parra taputjunama
yulama ngurrakutu.

That night she kept a big fire burning in her windbreak.
A little dove, her cousin Kurlukuku, came and sat
a little way from the fire. Then the fire started to make
a crackling noise and the emu asked her chicks,
"Children, what's that crackling noise?" She kept
hearing the noise and she kept on asking them,
"What's that noise?" She was crying
at the same time. It was only the fire,
because that bird sat next to it.

Then the little dove said, "Blind one!
Why are you crying, cousin?" And the
emu said, "I played a trick on the turkey.
I told her to kill her two chicks and so
she threw the seeds on my eyes.
That's why I'm blind."

And the little bird said, "I'll fix your eyes
with my maparn." So he fixed up the emu.
He gave her two special eyes. The dove
told the emu, "With this eye I'm giving you,
from a long way off you can see people
as if they were very close up. When you see
them, you will run away." That's why today
we see the emu's tracks on the ground,
still fresh, but the emu is long gone
before people come near.

Emus and turkeys are no longer seen
together; they are not friends. The emu
lives on her own, away from the turkey.
The turkey still has her twins, even today,
and if you have a close look at the emu's
eyes, there is still rough skin around them,
from where the seeds burnt her.
The turkey played a trick on the emu
to pay her back for what she had done.

Maparn is magic

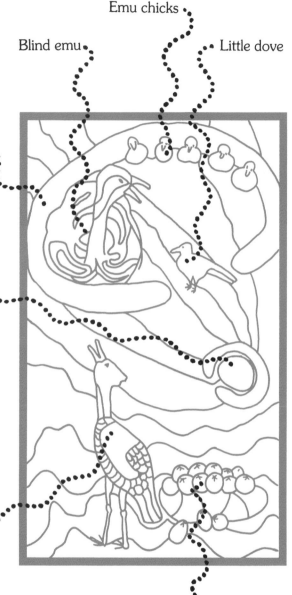

Emu chicks

Blind emu · Little dove

Windbreak

Fireplace

Turkey

Bush tomatoes

14

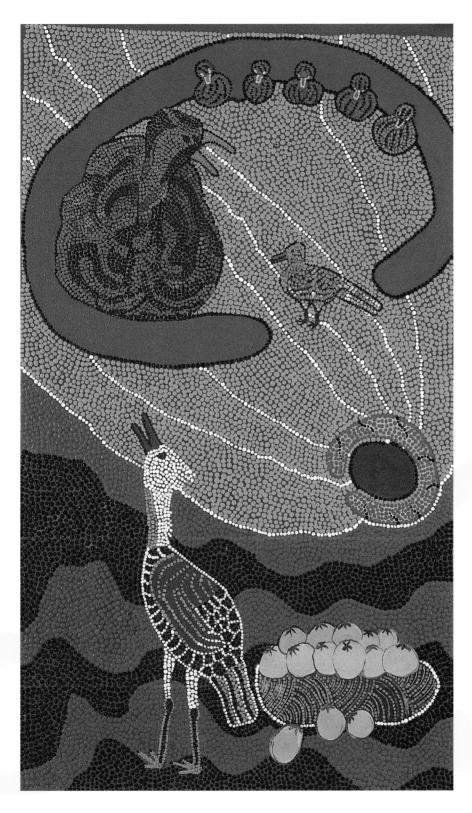

Tilirnu tjarlu-tjarlu
waru ngurrangka.
Yanamara parnkungurninytji
Kurlukuku. Yarltingura
palurukurnu tjiitjiku,
"Tjiitji, ngana tjiitja
warungka kinti,
ngana tjiitja?"
Kurlukuku wangkangu,
"Pampa, nganatjanun
yulinpa parnku?"

"Tirrutjunurnalu Kiparalu.
Watjarnuna pungkuwangku
tjiitji kutjarra. Wirrupungulpirni
kumpupatja paniyangka
tjiitjanulpina pamparringu."

Turrulu lamparntju
watjarnu, "Palyalku
nyangu paniya
maparnkurlu."
Palyarnura paniya
Karlayaku. Yungkurnanta
paniya mikutjanan
nyakuwa puntu
tiiwanguru.

Kipara
kamulungkupula
Karlayalu wiyangu
nyawa. Nyinalura
Karlaya tiiwa
Kiparangkamarra.
Kuwarri Kiparalu
kanyirnin tjiitji
kutjarra.

15

The Black Goanna

Walyparnku

In the Dreamtime, before he was black,
this goanna used to live on his own.
He didn't have a wife.
He saw that the other men all
had wives and he wanted one
too. The black goanna went
around asking each of the men
for a wife but they all said, "No!"
So he went walking
and thinking a long way
from their camp.

Kurralka Tjukurrtja,
Walyparnku nyinama
kutju kutju ngurrangka.
Wiya nyupa kanyirnma.
Nyangutjananya puntu
nyupalaltu. "Kurlu
nyupawiya palurulu
kanyirnma?" Walyparnkulu
tjapirnu yuwarrniya kutju tutju.
"Wiyaya." Yanu tiiwa
ngurrakutu.

Hole at the bottom of tree •

• Black goanna

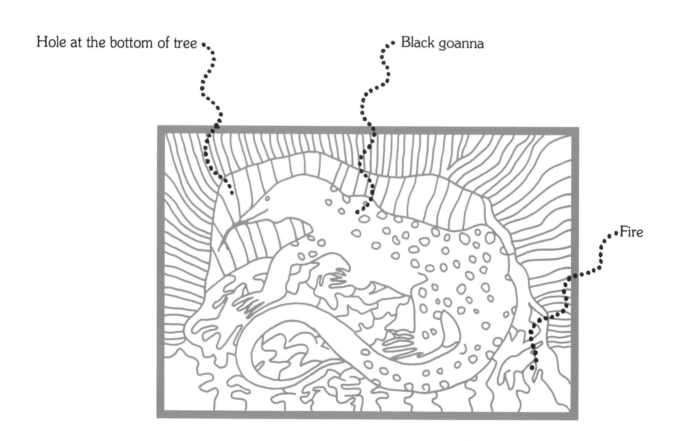

•Fire

16

He thought of a plan and he set up
his own camp in the bush.
One night he left his place
and went to one of the men's camp.
He crept in and took the man's
wife away with him. Every night
he went to another man's camp
and took that man's wife. He went
to every man's camp until he had
all of their wives. Some of the women
were his relations. He didn't care.
He even took his own mother-in-law!

Mungangkatjana yanu
kutju puntukutu
ngurrakutu. Yanura
tjarrpangu, ngurrangka
manu nyupa
katingu tiiwa.
Laltutjananya manama
tutju katjiya wiyarringu.
Kalkinparraya walytja
nyinama. Yumari
lurrtjungku manu
tawurnpungula katingu.

The mother-in-law taboo is described
in the section Stories and Kinship, p42

The men in the camps were angry. They all came together for a big meeting about this black goanna. The men asked each other, "What are we going to do with Walyparnku?" Every night they would see the black goanna dancing around his big fireplace, showing off with his stolen wives and making himself happy with them. Then one of the men said, "We should set fire to his camp while he's sleeping."

They all got their wives back while he was sleeping, until he was the only one left asleep in the windbreak. Then they lit a fire all around so he couldn't escape. The fire burnt right through to him. That's how come his skin is black, and that's why they call him, "Black Goanna always looking around".

Puntuya wirriyirringu nyinama. Wangkanguya nyaalpankula Walyparnku. Katji mungarriwa nyawaya katji nyarnpipuwa waruwana. Mikurrima ngulyukurlu nyupakurlu. Puntu kutju wangkangu, "Warula tililku katji nyarlirriku tjirntungka."

Katji nyarlirringu manutjananyaya marlaku nyupangartuka. Tilirnuya waru yirrpintu. Tjiitjanungkaltara yarnangungurra marurringu. Walyparnkupaltaya yinitjunu wulungalta.

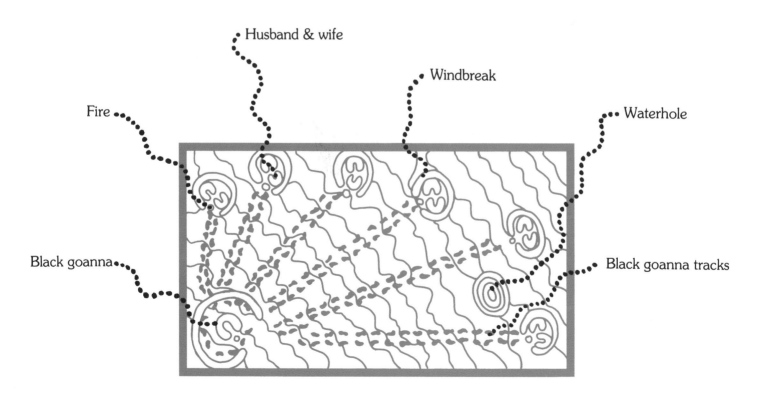

- Husband & wife
- Windbreak
- Fire
- Waterhole
- Black goanna
- Black goanna tracks

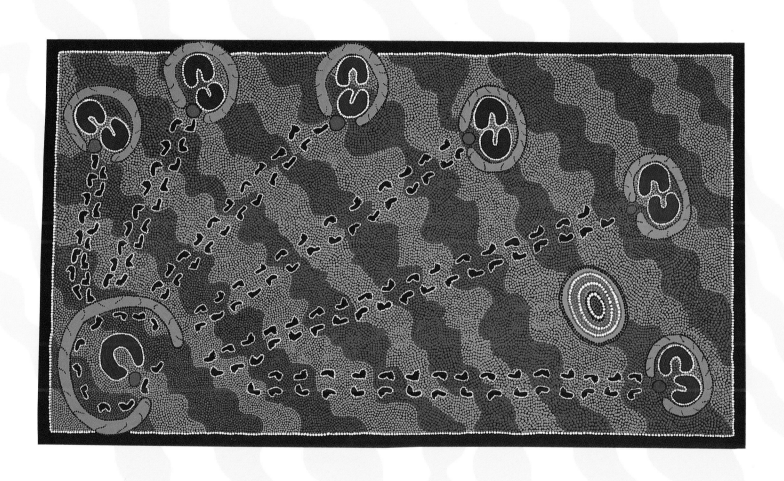

The Witchetty Grub Man Dreaming

This story starts around Lake Gregory.
Walmajarri people used to live there.
My grandfather's Dreaming comes from this story.

A long time ago, there were two
Snake men who were people
in the Dreamtime. They were brothers
but one got jealous. At that time
the people were having a big
corroboree. The jealous Snake man
'sang' his brother and made him change
into a snake. The snake
went into a lake called Kurntukurta
and he is still living in the lake today.
His name is Ngirntituti,
which means "short tail".

After this the jealous brother
went travelling south to a lake
called Mulatja.
When he got there,
he saw a lot of people
sitting around.

Lukuti Puntu Tjukurrpa

Ngaatja Tjukurrpa Malarntjanu.
Puntuya Walmajarri nyinama.
Ngayukunukura tjamiriku Tjukurrpa.

Tjukurrtapula nyinama
kurtararra lingka
kutjarra. Puntuluya
yinkarnma turlku.
Katjiya turlku
yinkarnu wiyarnu
kurtalungku kutjupalu
lingkamanu. Tjiitja
lingka yanu
Kurntukurtakutu.
Kuwarri wulu nyininpa.
Yinira Ngirntituti.

Kurta kutjupa yanu wilura Malarnkutu.
Katji yanu kintirringu nyangutjananya.
Kurta mingarr-mingarrpa
wurna yanu yurlpayirra
warranwana Mulatjakutu. Katji
ngarangu, nyangamatjana
puntu laltu katjiya nyinarrawananma.

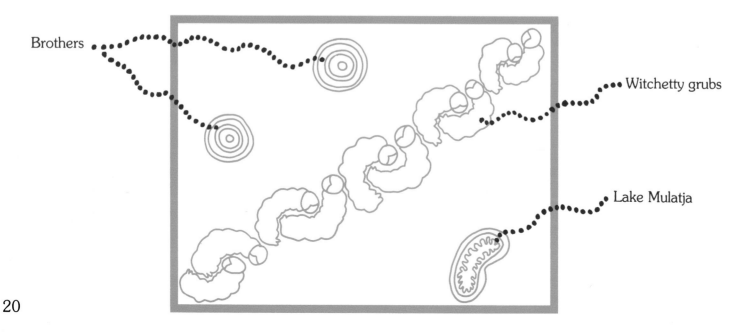

Brothers

Witchetty grubs

Lake Mulatja

20

All the people were sitting
down and looking at this stranger
who had come from a long way.
As soon as he sat down
they all began to cry
as they felt sorry for him.
No one knew him.

Puntuluya taranyangama
puntungka tjiingka
munuputungka. Puntu
tjiitja nyinakitjarrimalpi,
puntuluya yulama
yalurr-yalurrpa. Ngurrpaluraya
nyinama wiyara kutju
nintinyinama wiya.

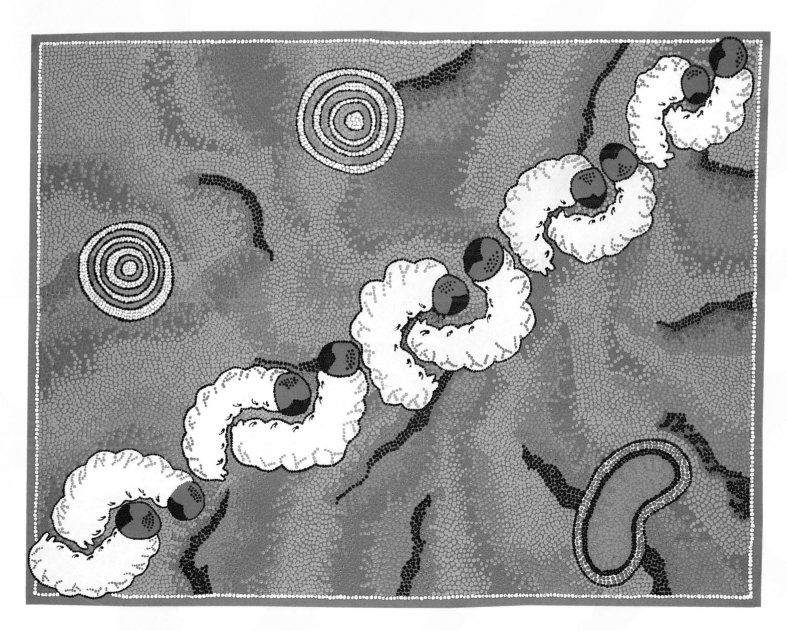

After they had finished crying with him,
he got up and kept walking south
until he came to another lot of people.
They were Witchetty people.
He was tired and could not go any
further so he stayed there with them.
He was so tired he could not move.

The people in the camp gave him food
when they came back from hunting.
And they told the man
he was not to leave their camp.
"Stay here, don't go away.
We want to see you still here
when we get back."

Yulanguya katji
wiyarringu puntu
tjiitja munupuntu
pakarnu yanu
ngurrakutjupakutu.
Yumpalyarrimalpi nyinangu
ngarringu tjiingkakirli.

Yungkamaraya mangarri
wartiltjanulu. Watjarnuraya
puntulu tjiintu, "Wiyan
wurna yanku nyuntu.
Nyina ngaangkakirli.
Yankulatjunta nyaku
marlakurrinytjalu."

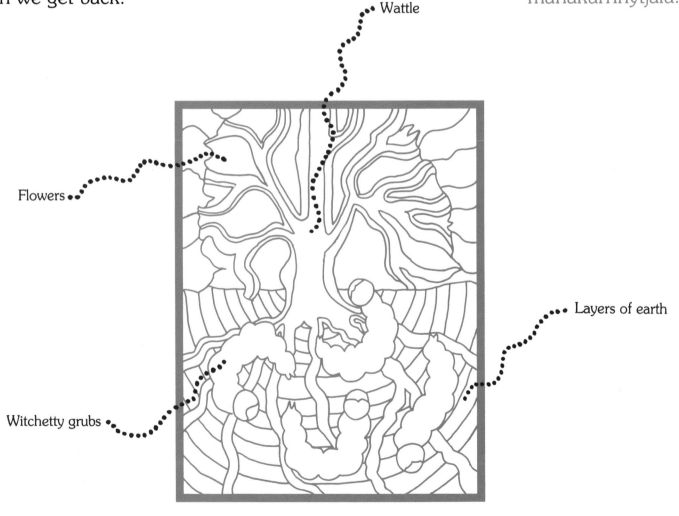

Wattle

Flowers

Layers of earth

Witchetty grubs

But he got up and walked off
while they were away. When the people
came back to camp, they looked for
the Snake man but he was not there.
They decided to punish that man for not
listening to them. Once before he had
been cheeky to an old Witchetty man.
Now that Witchetty man 'sang' him.
As he was travelling,
he tripped over a stick.
He was crawling like a caterpillar.

The Witchetty people followed
his tracks to where he was lying,
still trying to crawl.

"Get up! Try to walk," said an old man
with a coolamon. "I can't get up.
I'm too weak. I think I'll die right here,"
he answered.

Tiiwanypakirli nyinangu
pakara yanu. Wulukatji
parra yanama
palurulungku karlpirnulpi
wartangka. Puntulu
kutjulu yinkarnu,
yinkarnu katji
wayinmalpi lukutiyuru.

Puntu ngaanpangaya
lukutiyuruya nyinama.
Wananmaraya yiwarra katjiya
parlipungu wayintjakutu.

Puntulu kutjulu ngalura kanyirnma
luwanytja wangkarraka,
"Pakalakutjangku yarrkala wurnaku."
"Wiyarna pakalku
wiya yumpalyarringurna.
Mirrirrikurna ngaangakirli."

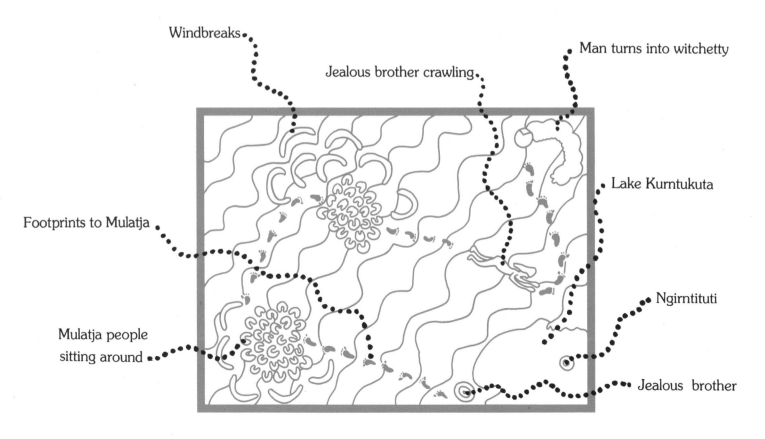

Windbreaks

Man turns into witchetty

Jealous brother crawling

Lake Kurntukuta

Footprints to Mulatja

Ngirntituti

Mulatja people
sitting around

Jealous brother

They were shaking him,
trying to wake him up,
but he was too tired. He changed
into a big rock the same shape
as a witchetty grub.
In that country when people die,
they change into witchetty grubs.
And there in the same place
white ghost gums grow now,
with plenty of witchetty grubs.

Manuya puntulunga
yurritjunama mikuya
kanalkuwa. Wulu ngarrima
yurriparni. Pamarryanulpi
kuwarringan nyaku lukutiyuru.
Ngurrangka tjiingka puntuya
katji mirrirri lukutiyurulpi nyina.
Wartaya tjarlu-tjarlu
ngurrangka tjiingkanya
Lukuti laltupi kuwarri.

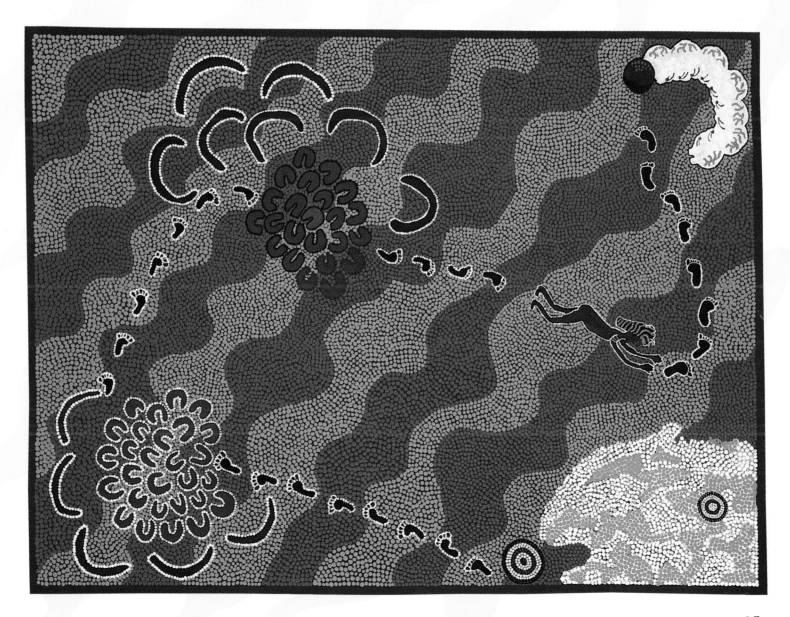

25

Kalpartu the Dreamtime Snake

The Dreamtime snake Kalpartu lives in the deep waters in rivers and lakes and rockholes. He is a spirit snake. When we take strangers or children to a waterhole or a swimming place for the first time, we tell them to throw in a rock so the snake can 'know' them.

If the snake doesn't know someone, he might get inside them and make them ill. Or he might come up from his resting place and make a whirlpool to pull the stranger under. The Dreamtime snake lives in the stars. Children who stare at the stars too much will find their hair turns white when they get older.

My mother told me the story of a waterhole called Tarnku. This is the story of Tarnku.

Kalpartu Tjukurrta Lingka

Tjukurrta Kalpartu nyina kalyungka. Wiyayuru nyina lingkayuru katjiya tjiitji yarra tupurlyarra. Lingka nyina kankarra. Wirrupuwalpiya tjiitjilu pamarrpa kalyungka, mikutjanampa nintinyinakuwa.

Katjiwiyaya wirrupuwa tjiitji tjiitja mirri punkala. Tjukurrtjanu lingka nyina kankarra. Katjiluya tjiitjilu nyawa kankarra wirlpangka, wiritjana pakala.

Ngayukunulu yipilu watjarnurni wangka kalyu Tarnku. Ngaatjangkura wangka Tarnkukulu.

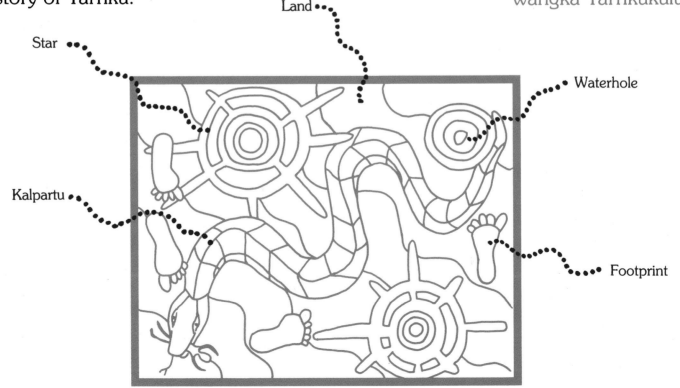

Land ••
Star ••
Waterhole
Kalpartu •
Footprint

In the Dreamtime this place was a ceremonial ground and the people were having a corroborree. The Willy Wagtail man came for a visit but the people tried to keep him out of the dances. They teased him and made him feel unwelcome.

Tulkuya kantunma laltuya yanama tulkuya pungama. Tjintirr-Tjintirr puntu yanamangkura matjarri yanama puntuluya ngunyipunguya. Tjiintuya yartjiyartjimanama. Kamuya watjarnuraya wiyarnyanamul.

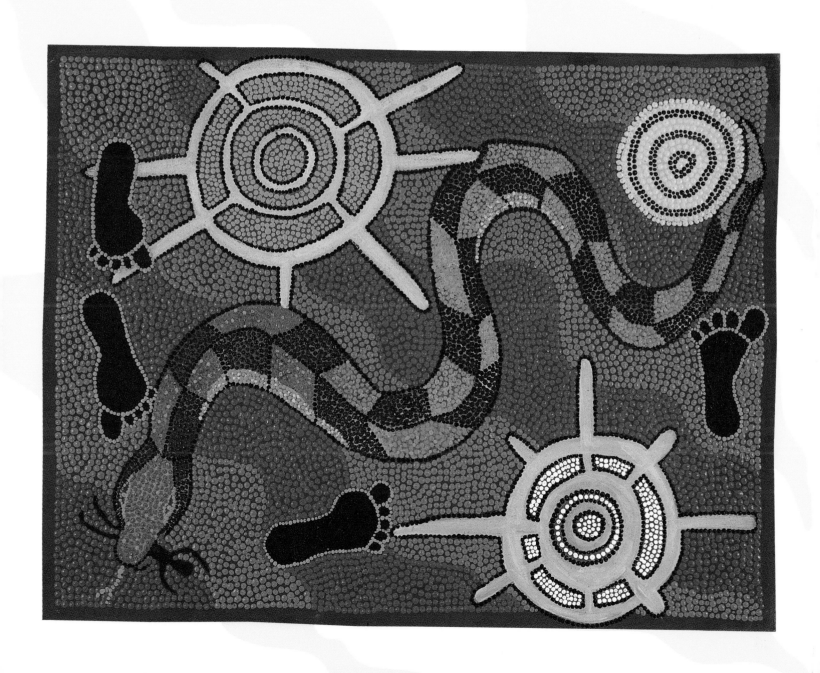

So Willy Wagtail man went
for help to his cousin brothers,
who were Dreamtime snakes.
And then along came those two
snakes, the Kalpartu, travelling
underground to this place, Tarnku.
They were travelling underground,
so they had to get up somewhere.
One of them got up at the main
rockhole and the other came
in from the left through
the gorge there.

You know what they did?
The snakes surrounded
the dancers. They made a big flood,
which killed all of the people
except for one, who changed into
a white corella. Now you can see
these white corellas.
They stay near the rockhole.
They are the people who lived there
in the Dreamtime.

Tjiitjanu Tjintirr-Tjintirr puntu
yanangkura parnkukunutjananya
kurralka tjukurrtjanu lingka. Tjiitjanu
tjiitjana yanamaraya kutjarra lingka,
kutjarra. Yanamapula
kaninytjarrawana ngurrakutupula
Tarnkukuta. Yanupula
kaninytjarrawana nyangupula
kaninyintjarrawana tjartuwanapula
pakalkuwa. Kutju yanu pakarnu
pamarrta kalyungka. Yanu
pamarrtawana pakarnu tjampukarti.

Nyunturan kurlu ninti nyaalpirringuya
kutjarra lingka yumurringutjana
tulkumayanta tjiitjanupula
palyarnu tjarlu kalyu mirringirri laltu.
Kutjulungku puntulu kiiparimanu.
Kuwarriltalu nyangun laltu
lipi kiipari. Kuwarriya kinti
nyininpa kalyu kinti. Tjiinpaya
tjiinpangkuraya puntu
nyinamangkuraya Tjukurrtjanu.

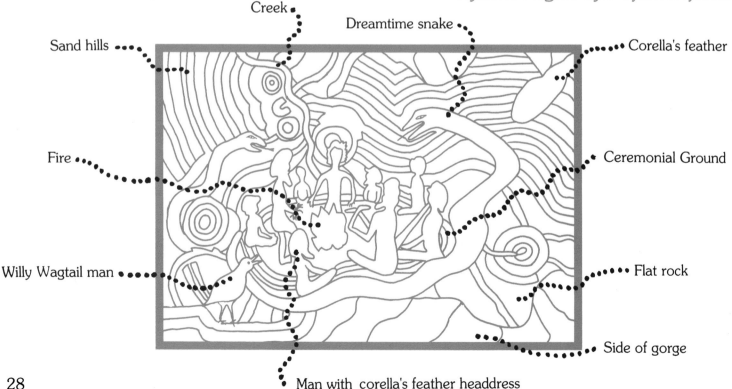

Creek

Dreamtime snake

Sand hills

Corella's feather

Fire

Ceremonial Ground

Willy Wagtail man

Flat rock

Side of gorge

Man with corella's feather headdress

28

Today the Kalpartu get
up from the waterholes
and travel through the sky
at dawn and dusk. They form
the long white clouds,
low in the sky.

When he's angry a Dreamtime
snake leaves his waterhole.
Thunderstorms and rain follow him.
When he has quietened down
we see his rainbow in the sky.

All this is still here today.

Kuwarri Kalpartu pakala kankarra
kalyutjanu yarra kankarrawana rakarra-
rakarra yulyultjarra kamu tjuturlpa.
Nganayimarrakuya tawarralungkuwa
lipiyungkura ngangkarli kanyintjarra
yalkirriwana.

Katjingkura wirriyirri Tjukurrtjanu lingka
wantingku kalyu. Mangirri kamu
kalyu wanalaya paluru. Katjingkura
yakari ngawalaya tjutirrangu
yalkarringka.

Ngaatjun nyakun kuwarri.

29

How the Emu Got Short Wings

A long time ago, the emu
bird lived in the sky.
His nest was on the clouds.
Every evening
from his nest he used
to watch the brolgas
dancing by the lake
and he loved their dance.
That emu was
wondering to
himself if he could
come down and
dance like them.

So one day he flew
down from his nest
to where the brolgas
were dancing.
Then he went among
them and asked the brolgas
to teach him their dance.

One of the brolgas said to him,
"Spread your wings out like this."
And then another one
of the brolgas said to the emu,
"Come on, dance like this,
the way we brolgas dance."
So he tried
but his wings were so big
they got in the way. That brolga
got angry and stopped the emu,
and shouted, "Spread your wings!"

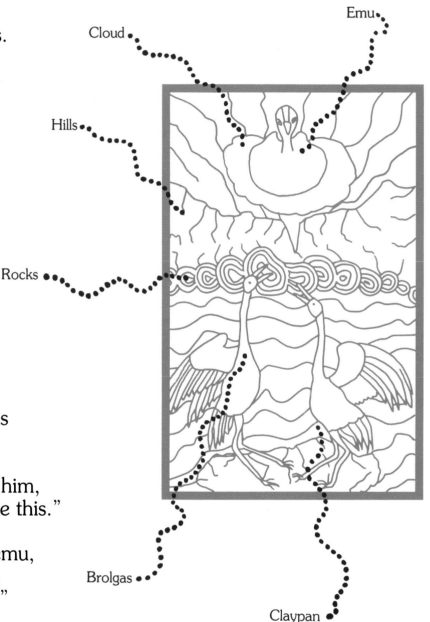

Cloud

Emu

Hills

Rocks

Brolgas

Claypan

Nyaalpakarralu Karlayalu Kanyirninpa Pinkirrpa Lamparnpa

Kurralka Karlaya nyinama kankarra ngarnkangka. Purlkura nyinama ngangkarlingka. Yuly-Yulytjarra nayangkura nyina purlkungka kamu nyawalu kaninytjarrawakulu Walanytjanga katji nyarnpipuwa warrankinti. Palurulunga kulinma, "Kurluparna tjarwitikuwana nyarnpipungku palunyayurulu?"

Tjirntungka kutjungka parrpakarnungkura purlkutjanu, yanulu nyinatingu Walanytja katji ngarala tjukurrpungama. "Ngururryanatjana!" Tjapirnutjana Walanytja, "Palyalurna nyarnpipungin kurlu?"

Walanytjulu kutjulu nintinma mikungku pinkirrpa yiyalkuwa. "Pinkirrpangku yiyala ngaaltjilu." Watjarnulpira, "Nyarnpipuwa ngaaltjilu ngayunyurulu." Ngarangukalu watjarnu Karlayangka, "Pinkirrpangku rapuwa."

31

There were a lot of brolgas there at the same time waiting
for that emu to spread his wings, so they could dance.
Then the emu spread his wings. They went right
over everybody, they covered all the brolgas
on the hill! When he did that,
all the brolgas got a fright
and fell on top of each other.

"No! no! no!" all the brolgas
shouted to the emu, "Your
wings are too big!
Too big!
We'll have to cut
them off and
make them small
like our size."

So all the brolgas got hold
of his wings — both sides.
They held the emu's wings tight
and one of the brolgas
got the sharpest stone axe and cut
the emu's wings to make them shorter.

But he cut them too short,
too low. When the brolgas told
the emu to spread his wings,
the emu tried but he couldn't
see his wings any more!
He got a fright and he was sad that
he had lost his wings. And he said
to the brolgas, "You tricked me!"

This was because the brolgas were jealous
of his big wings. Then he took off into the plains,
away from the brolgas and he is never seen near
the lake because the brolgas are his enemies.
That's why the emu has short wings. That's all. That's the finish.

Sky

Emu

Sand

Rocks

Brolga

Ngaralaraya nyangamara walanypalaltu mikungku rapungkuwa pinkirrpa. Manutjana karlayalu pulputjunu Walanytja katjiya nyinama pamarrwana. Katji tjiilanyarringu walanypaya laltu karratarrima kamu punkanmaya.

"Wiya! Wiya! Wiya!" parlmananamaluya Karlayakutu. "Tjarlulkangku nyuntuku pinkirrpangku, wiyalka tjarlu minyirri! Kurntalkulatjupulanya pinkirrkutjarra kurlu? Ngayunyurulpilta nyinamalpa palya."

Manulpiraya ngalunma pinkirrkutjarra. Ngalunuya kanyirnma marrkalu kamu kutjulu manu tjimarri, kurntanmapiraya pinkirrpa.

Kurntarnulpiya wangkama, "Wiyapalara kurntarnu ngawurnu." Purtungku Karlayalu yarrkanma nyarni parrpakalkuwa purtungku yarrkurnu wiya. Purtupulanya nyangama pinkirrkutjarrangka. Yulamalpi karrata kamungku wurrkulinma.

Watjarnunin, "Nyuntulu mayitjunu!" Karlaya yanu tiiwa tjantirringka nyinatingu. Wiya marlaku yanama ngulu nyinama. Nyaalpakarralu Karlayalu kanyirninpa pinkirrpa lamparnpa. Nyarmu.

The Seven Sisters

This is the Napaltjarri and Tjakamarra Dreaming.
The story starts from somewhere down south.

In the Dreamtime, the seven Napaltjarri
sisters often came down from the sky.
They used a very special hill
for a landing place. The seven sisters
had a secret passageway going into
the top of the hill. A cave inside the hill
was their home. The old men on the
earth didn't know the Napaltjarri were
camping nearby. At that time there
were no other women on the earth.

One day when they had come down
from the sky, the seven sisters walked
around on the ground, hunting for meat
and other bush tucker. They travelled
around together, killing their meat and
eating it as they were looking about.
But they always came back to that
special hill. One of the old men,
called Tjakamarra, was walking past
and he saw them.

Napaltjarri

Ngaatja Tjukurrpa Napaltjarri kamu Tjakamarrakurlu.
Ngaatja tjukurrpa yurlpayirrajanu.

Kurralka, walytjirringka
nyinamaya Napaltjarriwarnu
ngaangka. Paluruntuya
ngurra kanyirnma
kaninytjarra parnangka
palya minyirritjanampa
ngaatja ngurra
nyinama yaka
pamarrta
kaninytjarra.

Walyangka Napaltjarriwarnuya
parraya yanama wartilpa kukaku,
mangarriku kamu. Kukaya pungkura
ngalkuma parra yankura ka yanama
ngurrakutu tjiikutu pamarrkutu katjiya
pakara yanama nayakarra wartilpa.
Yirna-yirna tjiinpa wiyaraya ninti
nyinama tjiitjalkaya
Napaltjarriwarnulta nyinama
tjiingka ngurrangka.

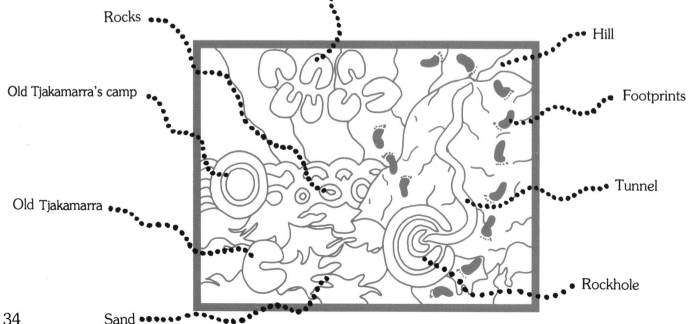

Seven sisters

Rocks

Hill

Old Tjakamarra's camp

Footprints

Old Tjakamarra

Tunnel

Rockhole

34   Sand

Tjakamarra came close to look,
as they drank the water from a creek
on the side of their hill. Old Tjakamarra
was creeping up to them. He wanted
to take one of the women to be his wife.
He was coming closer. He grabbed
the youngest sister!

Katjiya tjiinpa puntu wayintanama
wartilpuru. Nyangutjananya kutjulu
puntulu tjiilu yirnalu Tjakamarralu
parratjananya yanu kintilu
nyangama katjiya kalyili
tjikinma, nyangutjananya
yiyarnu karlkinpa.

When the other Napaltjarri saw
that he had hold of their youngest
sister, they started running into the
cave which was their home. They
climbed up the secret passageway
to the top of the hill. The six Napaltjarri
sisters took off into the sky
with their digging sticks.

The seventh sister was still struggling,
trying to get away from Tjakamarra.
That Napaltjarri girl was pushing him
away with all her might. She was biting
him hard on his hand, and hitting the old
man with her digging stick. Then that
girl bit the man really hard on his wrist.
He let go of her and she took off
into the sky after her older sisters,
telling them, "A man is following us!"

That's why they are all up in the sky.
They never came down again.
They are running away from old
Tjakamarra. He turned into
a big star called the Morning
Star. Today the seven sisters
are still in the sky and Tjakamarra
is there too. That's all!

Napaltjarri kutjungkura kamina
marlawanatjanu, pakarnu
wurnarringu, tjiilu puntulu
Tjakamarralu wanarnu wulukarra
wananma tjiitja Napaltjarri katji parra
yanulu kinti warinykatingulu
ngalurnu marumpunguru
mayaluminyirri wulu kanyirnma.

Napaltjarrilungkura
mayalu yurntunma
ka patjanma
marumpuwana
mayaluminyirri
katji yiyarnu
tjiitja tutju.
Napaltjarritjana taputjunu
warinykatingukatjana
watjarnu, "Puntululanya wanarninpa!"

Pakarnuya kankarra
tatirnu pamarrta
nyinama ngaralaka
wanangkuya manu,
ngaranguya pakarnupawana.
Nyanginpala
kuwarri Tjukurrtjanu
kuwarri. Nyarmu.

The Seven Sisters form the Pleiades constellation.

36

Kukatja country – Balgo

Stories and kinship

In our way, people sit down and listen to each other's word in turn, like you do. Do you like our stories?

Mary Djaru

The Tjukurrpa you have just read are often told among family groups after an evening meal. Their telling is a part of family life and helps to keep the culture and law of the Kukatja people. These stories, and the tracts of country they are connected with, belong to different kinship groups. The Roughtail Lizard Dreaming tells of how the stories were given as songs to the people, and is the starting point of the Kukatja family and kinship system, which is explained in the following pages.

The Kukatja family

Everyone born into a Kukatja family has a kinship or "skin" name as well as a given name. A girl's skin name begins with **N** and a boy's with **Tj**. Two examples are Nangala and Tjangala. Brothers and sisters are paired into eight skin groups, shown as large dots in diagram 1. In a particular family brothers and sisters belong to the same skin group. As an extended family everyone in one group calls each other sister or brother. All Nangala females are skin sisters of Tjangala males, all Tjapanangka are skin brothers of Napanangka. The pairs in each skin group are not marriage partners. A person finds a partner in an opposite group, as the green lines of the diagram show.

Nyupararra — Husband-and-Wife, Marriage

A skin name is kept throughout life and is very important. When a person marries there is one other group from which partners should be chosen. Such marriages are "straight skin" and are preferred. There are other groups into which it is forbidden to marry (the most critical of these is shown in diagram 7). Marriage with a forbidden partner would be "wrong skin" or "not tjugarni."

Diagram 1 shows the "straight marriage" lines. Tjampitjin men may marry Napangarti women, and Nampitjin women may marry Tjapangarti men. Because of the skin groups, all Tjampitjin men call Napangarti women nyupa, as do all Napangarti women call Tjampitjin men. They are like husbands and wives (nyupararra) to one another, with social obligations and roles, especially in caring for those in need. In the same way all Nampitjin and Napangarti women are like sisters-in-law (mantirri) and Tjampitjin and Tjapangarti men are brothers-in-law (makurnta). This applies to all the groups linked by the marriage lines.

Can you tell from which skin group Nungurrayi women accept partners if they are to marry "straight skin"?

What group is mantirri for a Napurrula woman?

nyupa: wife or husband
kurta: brother
tjutu: sister
makurnta: brother-in-law
mantirri: sister-in-law

Diagram 1

38

Tjiitji — Children
Yipi — Mother

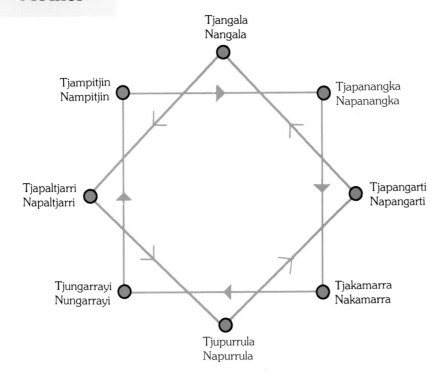

Tjangala
Nangala

Tjampitjin
Nampitjin

Tjapanangka
Napanangka

Tjapaltjarri
Napaltjarri

Tjapangarti
Napangarti

Tjungarrayi
Nungarrayi

Tjakamarra
Nakamarra

Tjupurrula
Napurrula

yipi: mother
mama: father
yurntal: daughter
yurntalpa: niece, nephew
katja: son
kamuru: uncle
lamparr: father-in-law
lamparr: son-in law

Diagram 2

Diagram 2 shows how to name the skin of the children (tjiitji). We look to the mother (yipi) to know the skin group of her tjiitji. The arrows lead from the yipi to her children. For example a Nangala mother will have Napaltjarri daughters (yurntal) and her daughters will have Napurrula daughters. Only after four generations will the yurntal again be Nangala. You can see from the diagram that there are two separate ongoing cycles of birth, each with its own direction.

As an exercise: can you name the skin of the tjiitji (girls and boys) of a Napanangka yipi?

Kamuru — Uncle
Yurntalpa — Niece, Nephew

The mother's brother will be the children's uncle. The arrows lead from the kamuru to his yurntalpa. If Nangala is the mother, her Napaltjarri and Tjapaltjarri children will have Tjangala uncles. The Nangala woman

has a Tjungarrayi husband, but his brothers, who are also Tjungarrayi, are *not* uncles to those Napaltjarri/ Tjapaltjarri children. Instead they are seen as fathers, in the social sense of an extended family. In the extended family Nakamarra women are seen as mothers for Tjungarrayi and Nungarrayi children, just as Tjapaltjarri men act as fathers to them, in matters of responsibility and social etiquette. This shows that you can always tell the skin name of a person if you know the skin of the mother, and vice versa.

If a boy is the yurntalpa of a Tjampitjin man, what skin was his yipi?

Lamparr — Father-in-law/Son-in-law

Diagram 2 also shows who a person's lamparr will be. The arrows lead from son-in-law to his father-in-law.

Who is the father-in-law of Tjapangarti?

Ngawatji — Paternal Grandmother/Grandchild
Kirlaki — Paternal Grandfather/Grandchild

Diagram 3

By combining diagrams 1 and 2 we can trace the paternal grandparents of any skin group. In diagram 3 we begin with a Tjungarrayi man and his Nangala wife, then trace forward through the male line of descent, starting with the children, who are Tjapaltjarri and Napaltjarri. That Tjapaltjarri son marries a Nakamarra woman and *their* children are Tjungarrayi and Nungarrayi. You can discover, as you continue to trace the male line of descent, that the skin name always "comes back" to where it started, so that the grandchildren carry the same skin name as their grandfather (the granddaughters have the matching skin name of that group).

How many generations in the male line does it take for the skin name to "come back"?

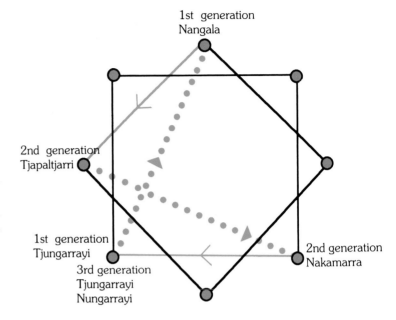

Mama — Father   Pimiri — Aunty
Tjiitji — Children   Yurntalpa — Niece, Nephew

By now you may be able to follow this diagram for yourself. The blue lines show the fathers of the children, the male descent lines. These lines also show the aunties of the children, since they are the sisters of the father and are grouped together with them. Nungarrayi women are aunties to Tjapaltjarri/Napaltjarri children.

What skin is the mama (this is the Kukatja word) of a Nakamarra girl?

Can you find the skin name of the pimiri of Napangarti or Tjapangarti tjiitji?

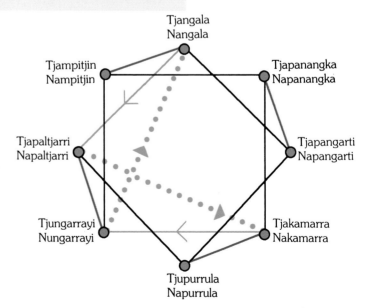

Diagram 4

40

Kaparli — Maternal Grandmother/Grandchild
Tjamu — Maternal Grandfather/Grandchild

Diagram 5

In diagram 5, the line from grandchildren to their maternal grandfather is the same as the line between cousins.

In the detail from diagram 5, you may see that grandchildren are directly opposite their maternal grandmother's skin group.

Can you find the skin group of the grandmother and grandfather of Tjupurrula/Napurrula?

(You could do this by tracing back three generations of female descent on the pink lines in diagram 2, starting with Napurrula.)

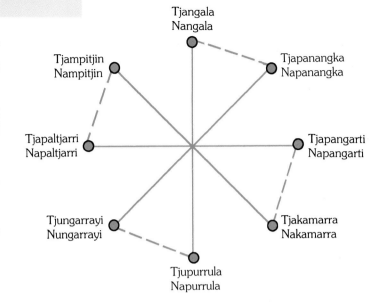

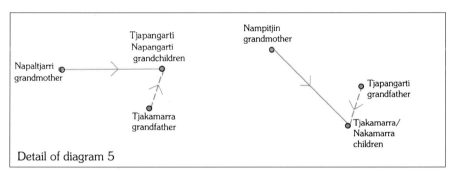

Detail of diagram 5

Parnku — Cousins

The orange lines show that Nampitjin/Tjampitjin persons are cousins of Napaltjarri/Tjapaltjarri. As an alternative to the preferred marriages of diagram 1, Kukatja people may choose to marry a person of a cousin's skin group, or a person from the same group as their maternal grandmother, shown in diagram 5. This is not a "straight skin" marriage, but children from such a marriage will always follow the normal pattern by deriving their skin group from their mother, as in diagram 2.

If a Napurrula has a Tjungarrayi for nyupa, she has married her skin-......?

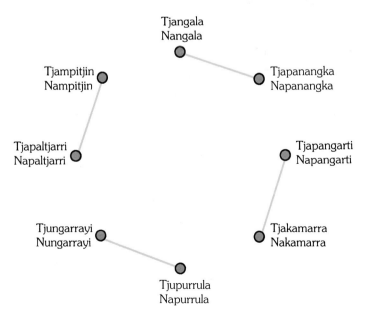

Diagram 6

Yumari — Mother-in-law/Son-in-law
Ngunyarri — Mother-in-law/Daughter-in-law

Diagram 7

The purple lines show the mother-in-law taboo. Yumari must avoid speaking to one another, or touching, or being familiar, or even looking at one another. In that way, the son-in-law should show respect for his mother-in-law. It is all right for daughters-in-law to have contact with mothers-in-law. The Black Goanna, in his story, does the wrong thing because he offends against this taboo: he even tries to marry his mother-in-law!

Can you tell the skin of Tjakamarra's yumari?

Was he "straight skin" or "wrong skin" for that Napaltjarri young woman?

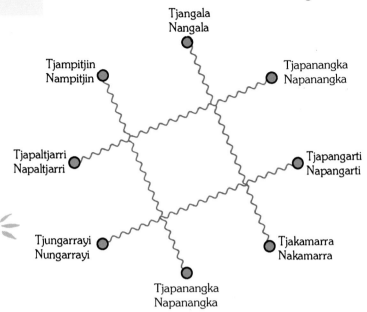

Tjangala
Nangala

Tjampitjin
Nampitjin

Tjapanangka
Napanangka

Tjapaltjarri
Napaltjarri

Tjapangarti
Napangarti

Tjungarrayi
Nungarrayi

Tjakamarra
Nakamarra

Tjapanangka
Napanangka

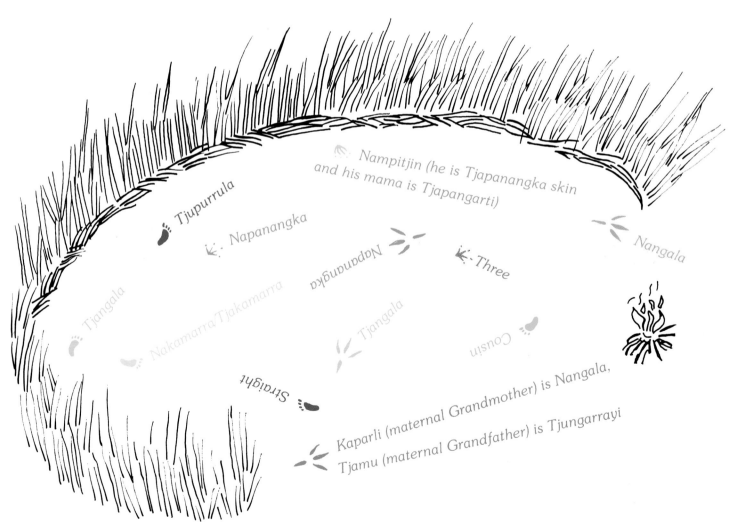

Tjupurrula

Nampitjin (he is Tjapanangka skin and his mama is Tjapangarti)

Napanangka

Nangala

Napanangka

Three

Tjangala

Nakamarra/Tjakamarra

Tjangala

Cousin

Straight

Kaparli (maternal Grandmother) is Nangala,
Tjamu (maternal Grandfather) is Tjungarrayi

42

Kukatja Pattern of Life

All these links between people can be combined into one diagram.

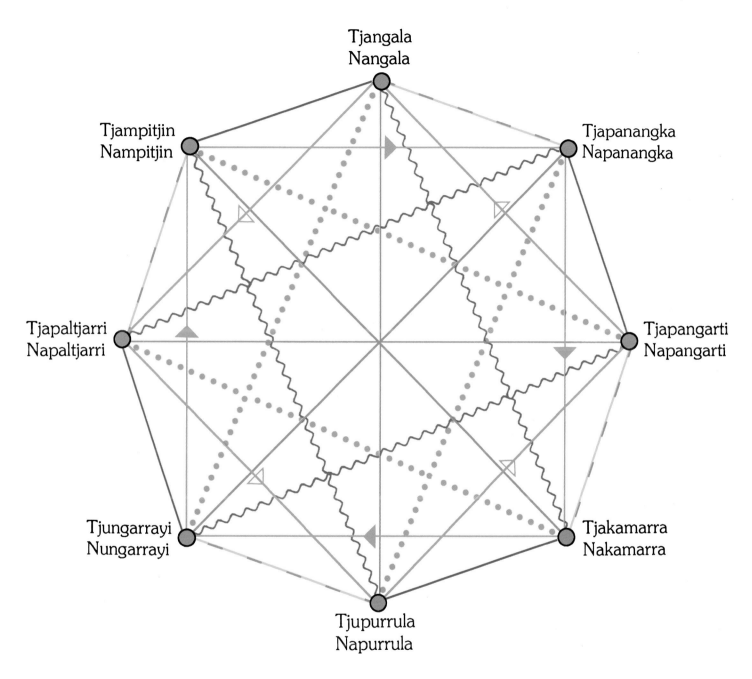

Diagram 8

Nyupararra	Marriage	Kaparli	Maternal Grandmother/Grandchild
Tjiitji — Yipi	Children — Mother	Tjamu	Maternal Grandfather/Grandchild
Kamuru — Yurntalpa	Uncle — Niece, Nephew	Parnku	Cousins
Lamparr	Father-in-law/Son-in-law	Yumari	Mother-in-law/Son-in-law
Ngawatji	Paternal Grandmother/Grandchild	Nyungarri	Mother-in-law/Daughter-in-law
Kirlaki	Paternal Grandfather/Grandchild		
Tjiitji — Mama	Children — Father		
Pimiri — Yurntalpa	Aunty — Niece, Nephew		

43

Notes on Kukatja

Adapted from Kukatja Language Handbook (Kimberley Catholic Education Language Team, Literature Production Centre, Wirrumanu 1991). Used by permission.

Today Kukatja is spoken by about 1000 people. Most live at Wirrumanu (formerly Balgo Mission), on the fringe of the Great Sandy Desert and roughly 260 kilometres south of Halls Creek, in the north of Western Australia. Wirrumanu is a little to the north-west of traditional Kukatja country. Kukatja is also spoken at Yaka Yaka, Malarn (Lake Gregory), Billiluna, Kiwirrkura, Lamarnparnta, Ngarantjadu, Ngirrpi, Piparr and Walkarli.

Children learn Kukatja as their first language at Wirrumanu, where Luurnpa School has a bilingual program. Kukatja is an oral language now being written with this orthography devised by linguists.

Some sounds used in Kukatja are the same as those in English, as are the letters used to write it, although some letters are also used differently. Tjarany, from the title of this book, is said with the **y** almost silent. As with English, some parts of words are not said as they are written (like the silent **k** in know), or are said in different ways (like the variation between **c** in circle and cage).

However, although not always said quite as it is written, in Kukatja each letter, or pair of letters, is used to write just *one* sound, and each sound is usually written in the same way whenever it occurs.

Many examples from the stories show that in Kukatja sometimes two letters are used for one sound, for example: Pipa**rr** and L**uu**rnpa, above. Similar cases in English are **th** in thin, **sh** in shin, **ea** in cream, **oo** in book, **ou** in out.

Vowel sounds

The vowels are a, aa, i, ii, u, and uu.

a	wana (stick), walya (ground)	Like the **u** in 'but'
aa	kaarnka (crow)	Like the **a** in 'father'
i	pimiri (aunt), mimi (sore)	Like the **i** in 'bit'
ii	tjiitji (child), tiiwa (far)	Like the **ee** in 'feet'
u	turru (bird)	Like the **oo** in 'book'
uu	luurnpa (kingfisher)	Like the **oo** in 'food'

Consonant sounds

The consonants are k, l, ly, m, n, ng, ny, p, r, rl, rn, rr, rt, t, tj, w, and y.

k	kipara (turkey) karlaya (emu)	Like the **k** in 'kid', but sometimes like the **g** in 'girl'
l	lukuti (witchetty) lungkurta (bluetongue)	Like the **l** in 'lip'
ly	kalyu (water) mulya (nose)	No exact match in English, see below
m	mangarri (food)	As in 'man'
n	ninti (know) nirrki (eaglehawk)	As in 'never'
ng	ngurra (camp)	As in 'sing'
ny	nyaku (look) nyanka (neck)	No exact match in English, see below
p	paniya (eye) pamarrta (on rock)	Like the **p** in 'pit', but sometimes like the **b** in bit
r	rapuwa (spread out) raka (five)	Like the **r** in 'rain'
rl	turlku (song) turlpu (heart)	No exact match in English, see below
rn	wurna (went) tjurni (stomach)	No exact match in English, see below
rr	mirrirri (die) mirru (spearthrower)	No exact match in English, see below
rt	tjampukarti (left) murti (knee)	No exact match in English, see below
t	lukuti (witchetty) tiiwa (far)	Like the **t** in 'top', but sometimes like the **d** in 'dog'
tj	tutju (girl) Tjangala (skin name)	Like **ch** in 'chair', but sometimes like the **j** in 'jam'
w	wiya (nothing) wirta (dog)	As in 'woman'
y	yipi (mother) yakarn (moon)	As in 'you'

Sounds you might find difficult

When Kukatja speakers learn English they often find some of the sounds unfamiliar to hear and say. In the same way, some Kukatja sounds are difficult for English speakers, either because of the way they are used, or because they have no exact match in English. If you don't make your Kukatja sound correctly it can affect the meaning, just as when saying 'shin' and 'chin' in English. As an example, in Kukatja 'marlaku' means *go back*, 'marluku' means *for kangaroo*.

A sound which is used differently in Kukatja: ng

Kukatja and English both use the letters **ng**, but unlike English, the Kukatja **ng** is always said the same way, as in the English word 'sing'. Never say it with a hard **g** as in finger. In English this sound is never used to begin words, but in Kukatja it can occur anywhere in a word. This means that you may find it a challenge to hear and say the **ng** sound to begin a word in Kukatja, for example: ngurra (camp).

Kukatja sounds which have no exact match in English: ly ny rl rn rr rt

In Kukatja, the pairs of letters **ly** and **ny** are used for only one sound each. It may help you to think of the sounds as a combination: **ly** is like an English **l** and **y** said simultaneously, as in 'million'; **ny** is like an English **n** and **y** said simultaneously, as in 'onion'. In Kukatja they are said as *one* sound, not two. English speakers may have difficulty hearing and saying these as single sounds, especially at the ends of words.

The sound **rl** is like the **l** in English, but is said by curling the tip of the tongue back past the ridge behind the top teeth. It sounds a little like an **r** followed by a **t** or **d**.

The sound **rn** is like the **n** in English, but is said by curling the tip of the tongue back past the ridge behind the top teeth. It sounds a little like an **r** followed by an **n**.

The sound **rr** is similar to the rolled **r** sound in Scottish English, and in other languages including Spanish and Indonesian. It is said by allowing the tip of the tongue to vibrate against the ridge behind the top teeth. However, sometimes this sound is made by just quickly 'flapping' the tip of the tongue against this ridge, and so it may sound more like a **d**.

The sound **rt** is like the **t** and **d** in English, but is said by curling the tip of the tongue back past the ridge behind the top teeth. It sounds a little like an **r** followed by a **t** or **d**.

More about saying Kukatja words

In English, if you change the stress on a word you can change its meaning (for example: re*cord* and *rec*ord, per*mit* and *per*mit). In Kukatja, like many Aboriginal languages, stress is not used in this way. Instead, the main stress usually falls on the first syllable of the word, for example: *ngu*rra, *pim*iri, *pu*ngama.

A 'consonant blend' is when two or more consonant *sounds* occur together. In English, consonant blends containing three or more consonant sounds are quite common, for example: **str spr skr sks sts**. Unlike English, blends of three consonant sounds or more are very unusual in Kukatja, and never occur at the beginning of a word.

Kukatja words always begin with a consonant sound, and vowels only occur in the middle and at the end of words. They usually have at least two syllables, unlike English, in which words of one syllable are very common.

Kukatja is a 'suffixing language'. Suffixes are parts of words added to build on the meaning. For example:

> pinkirrpa – wings
> pinkirrkutjarra – two wings
> pinkirrtjarrangka – on the two wings

This is why there are so many large words in the Kukatja versions of the stories.

A note about -pa

Lots of Kukatja words end in **-pa**. Kukatja favours vowel endings, so when there are words that end in a consonant, a **pa** will often be added. Luurn will become luurnpa, pamarr will become pamarrpa. It may even be used when an English word occurs in a Kukatja conversation, for example: 'Helenpa'. Try this out on your own name if it ends in a consonant. That is what you would be called among Kukatja speakers, say at Yaka Yaka or Billiluna.

More than one way to speak Kukatja

Kukatja, like any other language, has more than one dialect, and appropriate level of usage. Some Kukatja speakers may say words differently, or choose from a variety of words to refer to the same thing. Some Kukatja speakers say 'kumpupatja' and others say 'kumpupapatja' for 'bush tomato'. It is a living and changing language.

Kukatja word list

Many of these meanings are strongly influenced by the particular context of the stories. Capitalised names of animals in this list refer to Spirit beings.

ka	relates elements of a sentence, often signifying repetition of the behaviour. With *yanama:* going back again, with *patjama:* biting repeatedly 5,34,36
Kaarnka	crow (vi),5,6,7,44, *inside back cover*
Kaarnkalu	crow did 7
Kaarnkalura	the crow did (something) for him 5,6
kakarra	east 4,10
kakarralu	from the east 4
kalkinpa	other *title page* (ii), *i.b.c.*
kalkinparraya	other lot 17
Kalpartu	spirit snake, rainbow serpent (v,vi,vii),26,29, *i.b.c.*
kalyili	north 35
kalyu	water 4,26,28,29,44
kalyungka	in water 2,5,26,28
kalyungurulu	from water 5
kalyutjanu	out of the water 29
kamina	young girl 36
kampangu	burnt 13
kamu	with (linking or binding by association) (vi),5,10, 13,29,31,33,34, *i.b.c.*
kamulungkupula	those two, together (doing together) 15
kamulupulanyaya	and they them were (keeping) 10
kamungku	she then, herself (was doing it) 33
kamuru	uncle 39,43
kamuya	and they 27
kanalkuwa	to wake him up 25
kaninytjarra	beneath (down below, underneath) 5,7,29,34
kaninytjarrawakulu	looking down, underneath 31
kaninytjarrawana	underground 28
kankarra	above 5,6,26,29,31,36
kankarrawana	gets on top, goes above 29
kankarrawanalu	above, on top 5
kantunma	stamped (feet) 27
kanyila	to keep it 4
kanyirnin	keeping 4,6,7,15
kanyirninpa	possesses (vi),10,12,31,33
kanyirnma	kept it, keeping 10,16,24,33,34,36
kanyirnu	kept 5
kaparli	paternal/maternal grandmother 41,42,43
kapula	there are two 5,12
Karlaya	emu (vi),10,13,15,31,33,44, *i.b.c.*
Karlayaku	belonging to emu, of the emu 15
Karlayakutu	towards emu 33
Karlayalu	the emu did (vi),10,12,15,31,33, *i.b.c.*
Karlayalupulanya	emu from these two 10,12
Karlayalura	emu (he the ...) 12
Karlayangka	on emu 12,13,31
Karlayangkura	belonging to emu 12,13
Karlayapula	emu together (making two) 10
karlkinpa	the others 35
karlpirnulpi	tripped over 24
karrata	frighten 33
karratalu	frightened 7
karratarrima	getting frightened 33
kata	head 12
katingu	took, keep (away) 17
katja	son 39
katji	when 8,13,18,20,22,24,25,31,33,36
katjiluya	if they 26
katjin	when you 4
katjinanyurranya	when I (put) this 4
katjinkura	when he became 29
katjipula	when they were 5
katjiraya	when they are 5,13
katjirra	if he does 13
katjiwiyaya	when they don't 26
katjiya	when they 5,12,17,20,24,26,33,34,35
kawurnwana	on the ashes 8
kayililu	from the north 4
kiipari	little corella 28
kiiparimanu	became a little corella 28
kilikikutu	to the creek *(kiliki)* 7
kilikiwana	along the creek 5
kinti	close to 13,15,28,36
kintilu	close to 35
kintirringu	getting closer 20
Kipara	turkey 10,15,44, *i.b.c.*
Kiparakurnu	for the turkey 12
Kiparalu	turkey has, still has (vi),12,15
Kiparalukangku	turkey started hitting herself 12
Kiparalulkapulanya	the turkey had them 10
Kiparalupulanya	then the turkey 10
Kiparanga	turkey went 10
Kiparangkamarra	away from the turkey 15
Kiparangkura	that turkey 12
Kiparapula	turkey both (it and the other mentioned) (iv),10
kirlaki	paternal grandmother 40,43
Kitji	middle part of Lake Gregory 1
Kiwirrkura	a community 44
kuka	meat 6,7
kukaku	for meat 34
Kukatja	a language, culture, people *title page* (iii), (iv,v,vii),37,38,40,43,44,45,46,47
Kukatjungka	to do with Kukatja (vi)
kukaya	meat they (were killing) 10
kulinma	listening (also question: are you listening?) 2,6, 12,31
kulinuya	they heard 2
kumpupatja	bush tomato 13,15,45
kumpupapatja	bush tomato 45
kurlu	isn't it so? (he) asked them 16,28,31,33
kurlun	are you? 6

Kurlukuku	dove 15, *i.b.c.*	lungkurta	bluetongue lizard 44
kurluparna	am I going to? will I really? (with purpose) 31	lurrtjukirli	together 10
Kurnkangalku	he ate it raw *(kurnka)*, common name for eagle: raw meat eater) (vi),5,8, *i.b.c.*	lurrtjungku	he also 17
		luurnpa	kingfisher, also name of school at Wirrumanu (iv),44,45
Kurnkangalkulu	also common name for eagle 5,6,7,8	luwanytja	coolamon 13,24
Kurnkangalkungka	on the eagle (putting lies to him, in this case) 6		
kurntalkulatjupulanya	cut the wings off 33	makurnta	brother-in-law 38
kurntanmapiraya	so they started cutting 33	Malarn	a place and community; white gum tree, where witchetties *(Lukuti)* are found (iv,v),1,44
kurntarnu	cut 33		
kurntarnulpiya	then they cut it 33	Malarnkutu	towards Malarn 20
Kurntukurta	part of Lake Gregory (scene of *Lukuti* story) 1	Malarntjanu	from Malarn 20
Kurntukurtakutu	towards Kurntukurta 20	mama	father (also *tati* from Kriol) 39,40,42,43
kurralka	long ago 2,5,10,16,28,31,34	manama	getting 5,13,17
kurta	brother 20,38, *i.b.c.*	mangarri	food 22,44
kurtalungku	the other brother 20	mangarriku	for food 34
kurtararra	brothers 20	mangirri	lightning 29
kutjarra	two 5,10,15,20,28, *i.b.c.*	mankuwarna	I want to get that 5
kutjarraku	for two or two of them 12	mantirri	sister-in-law 38
kutju	one 2,16,17,18,21,28	manu	got 4,5,8,12,13,17,33,36
kutju kutju	one by one 16	manulpiraya	they got those 33
kutjulu	one did (stress on one) 24,31,33,35	manutjana	they got it (with intent, purpose) with *pulputjunu:* (he) got (them) covered 33
kutjulungku	one only 28		
kutjun-kutjunpa	one by one 4	manutjananya	got them to 3
kutjungka	in the one (at the same time) 10,31	manutjananyaya	they got 18
kutjungkapula	two in one (place) 5	manuya	they got 25
kutjungkarringu	at once together 2	maparnkurlu	with magic 15
kutjungkura	for one (person) 36	marlaku	come back or go back 5,6,13,18,33,45
kutjupa	another one 8,20	marlakurrinytjalu	when we come back 22
kutjupalu	the other did 20	marlawanatjanu	the last person, the one behind 36
kutjupangurra	another one 4	marluku	for kangaroo *(marlu)* 5,45
kutjupatjanulu	to or from another, passing something on 4	marlukuran	for kangaroo 6
kutjuwarra	altogether (the whole lot) (vi),3	marnkalta	in the spinifex/grass 12
kutunngarringu	was sleeping 13	marrkalu	hard, (holding) tightly, to grip 33
kuturu	fighting stick 12	marumpu	hand 5
kuturukurlu	with the stick 12	marumpunguru	by the hand 36
kuwarri	today 4,15,20,25,29,36	marumpuwana	on the hand 36
kuwariltalu	now, today 28	marurringu	became black 5,8,18
kuwarringan	up till today 25	matjarri	visiting 27
kuwarrirnanyurranya	today this on you (I'm putting) 4	mawuntu	white paint 3,4
kuwarriya	now they are 28	mawuntulu	with white paint 4
		mayalu	hard 36
laltu	a lot 5,10,20,28,33	mayaluminyirri	very hard 36
laltulu	a mob, or the lot, big mob (did) 4	mayankurna	I'm going over 5
laltupi	big mob 25	mayi	food 6
lalturringu	became a lot 5,13	mayitjunama	lying 6,8
laltutjananya	taking the lot 17	mayitjuninparni	telling me lies 6
laltuya	a lot of them 27	mayitjunu	tricked me 33
Lamarnparnta	a community 44	mayitjurra	tell a lie 6
lamparnpa	shortened (*lamparn:* small) (vi),31,33	mikungku	became jealous 31,33
lamparntju	the little one did 15	mikuputarri	loveliest, most delightful 10
lamparr	father-in-law 39,43	mikurrima	love it, preening, becoming happy 18
lingka	snake (vi),20,26,28,29	mikutjanampa	envies, hates 26
lingkamanu	became a snake 20	mikutjanan	envy, hate 15
lingkayuru	like a snake 26	mikuya	so they can, in order to 25
lipi	white 28	mimi	sore 44
lipiyungkura	they are (possess) white 29	mingarr-mingarrpa	filled with disgust 20
Lukuti	witchetty grub (vi),20,25,44, *i.b.c.*	minyirri	very 6,33
lukutinguwawana	witchetty grubs under the ground *i.b.c.*	minyirripula	only two, outstanding pair 10
lukutiyuru	like a witchetty grub 24,25	minyirritjanampa	only one, special place, singularly special 34
lukutiyurulpi	they became like a witchetty grub 25	mirri	dead 5,26
lukutiyuruya	they are like witchetty grubs 24		

mirringirri	caused to die 28	nganatjanun	what's wrong (what's causing)? 15
mirringu	is dead 12	nganayimarrakuya	they changed themselves 29
mirrirri	die 25,44	ngangkarli	clouds 29
mirrirrikurna	going to die 24	ngangkarlingka	on the clouds 31
mirrkaku	for food 5	ngarala	let's stand there 31
mirru	woomera, spear-thrower 44	ngaralaka	let's (keep) stand(ing) 36
Mulatjakutu	to Mulatja (a place) 20	ngaralaraya	let's stand up and hold them (wings) 33
mulya	nose 44	ngarama	standing 5
mungakutjupa	other night, night time, black of night 2	ngarangu	stood 20
mungakutjupangka	on the other night 2	ngarangukalu	he stood for it (waiting) 31
mungangkatjana	at night 17	ngaranguya	they stood 36
mungarriwa	when it becomes night 18	Ngarantjadu	outstation community (means man standing), via Wangkatjungka (SE) 1,44
munupuntu	another man, from another tribe, stranger 22		
munupuntungka	from the stranger 21	ngarnkangka	in the sky 31
murti	knee 44	ngarrima	lying down 25
		ngarringu	lay 22
Nakamarra	one of the eight female skin groups 38-43	ngarrkangka	in (the) chest 4
Nampitjin	one of the eight female skin groups 38-43	ngarrkawana	around or across the chest 3
Nangala	one of the eight female skin groups 38-43	ngawalaya	look for him (it) 29
Napaltjarri	one of the eight female skin groups 38-43	ngawatji	paternal grandmother or grandchild 40,43
	collective name of star formation, the Seven Sisters, Pleiades, also applies to each Sister (vi),34,36	ngawurnu	made it no good, rubbish 33
		ngayuku	mine 6,7
		ngayukunukura	(this is) my own 20
Napaltjarrilungkura	that Sister 36	ngayukunulu	my own 26
Napaltjarritjana	the Sister doing something (she is running) 36	ngayukurnu	my one, mine 3
Napaltjarriwarnu	the Seven Sisters 34	ngayulu	myself 12
Napaltjarriwarnulta	group of girls there but unnoticed 34	ngayulurnatjana	I'm going to or I will so do so (stress on will) 12
Napaltjarriwarnuya	all the Sisters together, the whole lot 34	ngayunyurulpilta	he's become like us 33
Napanangka	one of the eight female skin groups 38-43	ngayunyurulu	like me 31
Napangarti	one of the eight female skin groups 38-43	ngayurna	me (as for me) 5
Napurrula	one of the eight female skin groups 38-43	Ngirntituti	short tail 20
nayakarra	always and forever, over and over 5,6,34	Ngirrpi	a community 44
nayakarralu	all the time 4,6	ngulu	frightened 33
nayangkura	always 31	ngulyukurlu	stolen 18
ngaakutjarra	these two 12	ngunyarr	mother-in-law/daughter-in-law 42,43
ngaaltjilu	what did he do with it? 31	ngunyipunguya	expelled, sent him packing 27
ngaangka	here 34	ngurlungkura	he's frightened 13
ngaangkakirli	stay here 22,24	ngurra	camp 4,34,44,45
ngaanpa	these title page (ii),4, i.b.c.	ngurrakutjupakutu	each to their own camp 22
ngaanpangaya	these are, these people 24	ngurrakutu	to the camp 5,6,10,12,13,16,17,34
ngaantu	these (this) lot 4	ngurrakutupula	the camp of those two 28
ngaatja	this 4,7,10,20,34	ngurrangka	at the camp 5,15,16,17,25,34
ngaatjananta	this thing (this Dreaming I'm giving to you) 3	ngurraraya	home country (vi)
ngaatjangkura	this belongs to 26	ngurratjanulu	from (her) camp 12
ngaatjun	all this 29	ngurrpaluraya	they don't know him 21
ngalangu	ate it 5	ngururryanatjana	went in the middle 31
ngalku	eater (Kurnkangalku: raw meat eater, eagle) 6	ninti	know 28,34,44
ngalkuma	was eating 7,34	nintinma	showing (making known) 31
ngalkunma	eating (with warungka: eating by the fire) 7	nintinyinakuwa	so he can know 26
ngalkura	eat for him 5	nintinyinama	he knew 21
ngalula	hold it 6	nintitjunkurnanyurranya	I'll show this to you 3
ngalunma	were holding 33	nintitjunutjananya	he showed them 4
ngalunuya	they held it 33	nintitjurra	show 2
ngalura	was holding (him by the wrist, to get him up) 24	nirrki	eaglehawk 44
ngaluratjunama	catching and putting 5	Nungarrayi	one of the eight female skin groups 38-43
ngalurnu	hold 36	nyaalpakarralu	why has? (vi),5,33
ngalyalpiya	towards 12	nyaalpankula	how will we? 18
Ngamarlu	rockhole near Wirrumanu (Balgo) 1,4	nyaalpankurnapulanya	what am I going to do with them? 12
Ngamarlungka	at Ngamarlu rockhole 2	nyaalpirringuya	what they (those) 28
ngana	what 15	nyaku	look, to see 4,22,25,44
nganakurnin	what for are you (why are you)? 7	nyakun	can be seen 29

48

nyakunara	will look for him 5
nyakuwa	to look at already 15
nyangama	looking 13,33,35
nyangamara	(she) was looking (with *yakalu*: looking quietly, peeping) 12,33
nyangamatjana	(he) was looking at them 20
nyanginpala	we will be looking 36
nyangu	saw 7,10,12,15
nyangulu	he saw 12
nyangun	can be seen 28
nyangupula	those two saw (they knew) 28
nyangutjananya	saw them 16,20,35
nyanka	neck 44
nyankawana	around the neck 12
nyarlirriku	when he's sleeping 18
nyarlirringu	when he went to sleep 18
nyarmu	no more 33,36
nyarni	tried to 33
nyarnpipungin	dancing, am I dancing (correctly)? 31
nyarnpipungku	to dance 31
nyarnpipuwa	dancing 18, get up and dance (exhortation) 31
nyawa	look 5,15,26
nyawalu	he was looking at 31
nyawatjutjana	to look at (with purpose) 10
nyawaya	they see (him) 18
nyina	sit 22,25,26,31
nyinakitjarrimalpi	wondering if he could sit down 21
nyinalura	stays away! (emphasis on separation) 15
nyinama	staying/sitting (in a place); also: stay, sit down! 2,5,10,13,16,17,18,20,21,24,31,33,34,36
nyinamalpa	be staying/sitting 33
nyinamangkuraya	they were staying/sitting 28
nyinamapula	they (always two) were staying/sitting together 5
nyinamaya	they were staying/sitting 34
nyinangu	sat/stayed 22,24
nyinanguya	they stayed (sitting down) 2
nyinarrawananma	sitting around 20
nyinatingu	sat down 31,33
nyinatingutjananya	he sat down in order to 13
nyinatjunu	made (them) sit down 3
nyininpa	sitting down 20,28
nyirntjiwana	around the waist 5
nyuntu	you 22
nyuntulu	you (plural) 33
nyuntuku	your 33
nyuntun	you are 5,6
nyunturan	do you? 28
nyupa	wife, girlfriend 16,17,38,41
nyupakurlu	another's wife 18
nyupalaltu	lot of girlfriends 16
nyupangartuka	their wives 18
nyupararra	husband and wife, marriage 38
nyupawiya	no wife 16
paarnutjananya	he made them cooked (*paarnu*), emphatically 5
pakala	get up 26,29
pakalakutjangku	get up by yourself 24
pakalku	get up 24
pakalkuwa	to get up 28
pakara	getting up 6,24,34

pakaraya	they get up 2
pakarnma	will you get up? 5
pakarnu	got up, went 5,12,13,22,28,36
pakarnupawana	came out through 36
pakarnuya	they got up 2,36
palunyalu	he/she did 5
palunyalutjananya	he himself was 5
palunyangka	then (he) on to (the ashes) 8
palunyayurulu	like them 31
paluru	him/her (that person) 5,29
palurukurnu	he/she for her own 15
palurulu	him/her did 5,16
palurulunga	he of himself (as in thinking, asking) 31
palurulungku	he himself 24
paluruntuya	they 34
palya	good 5,10,33,34
palyalku	make good 15
palyalurna	good, correctly 31
palyaminyirri	very good 2
palyarnu	made, caused to happen 28
palyarnura	they made it good 15
pamarrkarratjaku	among the hills (and of them) 5
pamarrkutu	to the hill 5,6,34
pamarrpa	the rock (*pamarr*) 26,45
pamarrpanga	that rock 12
pamarrta	on the rocks 28,34,36,44
pamarrtawana	around the hill 28
pamarrwana	around the rock or hill 5,33
pamarryanulpi	turned into rock 25
pampa	blind 15
pamparringu	became blind 15
paniya	eye 13,15,44
paniyangka	in the eye 13,15
pankarrpari	goanna 6
parlipungu	found (something) 24
parlmananamaluya	they were shouting 33
parnangka	on the ground, earth 34
parnku	cousin 15,41,43
parnkukunutjananya	to his cousins (purpose implied) 28
parnkungurninytji	your only cousin 15
parra	about and around (when looking) 6,7,8,13,24,34,36
parraran	around 5
parratjananya	went about 4,35
parraya	(they were) going around, (with yanama) walking around 34
parrpakalkuwa	to fly 33
parrpakarnungkura	he flew off 31
patjanma	was biting 36
pimiri	aunt 40,43,44,45
pinkirrkutjarra	two wings 33,45
pinkirrkutjarrangka	on the two wings 33,45
pinkirrpa	the wings (vi),31,33,45, *i.b.c.*
pinkirrpangku	wings are 31,33
Piparr	a community 44
pirrinma	scratching 13
pirrinmangku	rubbed 13
pulputjunu	covered them 33, *i.b.c.*
pungama	to dance 27,45
pungkura	hit (her) 7,34
pungkuwangku	told to hit (them), to kill them 15

Tjukurrtapula	in the Dreamtime together 5,20	wanarnu	followed 36
Tjukurrtja	in the Dreamtime 2,16	wangka	word, story, talk, language *title page* (ii),(vi),
Tjukurrtjanu	from the Dreaming *title page* (ii),26,28,29,36,		26, i.b.c.
	i.b.c.	wangkama	was talking 33
tjumangkarni	the beginnings, origins (vi)	wangkangu	talked 15,18
tjunamatjananya	he was putting (*tjunama*) on them 3,4	wangkanguya	they said (to themselves) 18
Tjungarni	"straight skin", correct kin relationship	wangkapayi	storyteller (vi)
Tjungarrayi	one of the eight male skin groups 38-43	wangkarraka	told him 25
tjuninpa	putting it 4	Wangkatjungka	a place, community, language and a people's
tjunku	going to put 3,4		name (v,vi),1,53
tjunulu	put it on 13	wantingku	leaves behind 29
Tjupurrula	one of the eight male skin groups 38-43	warinykatingukatjana	when she came out, appeared to the others 36
tjurni	stomach 44	warinykatingulu	came out, appeared 36
tjutirrangu	rainbow 29, *i.b.c.*	warrankinti	close to the claypan 31
tjutu	sister 38	warranwana	along the claypan 20
tjuturlpa	dusk 15	wartangka	on or over the stick 24
tulkumayanta	while they were dancing 28	wartaya	the trees 25
tulkuya	those dancers 27	wartilpa	was walking 10,34
tunkulpakarrpirnungku	hairstring tied around 5	wartilpuru	during the walkabout 35
tupurltjunu	dipped (him) 8	wartiltjanulu	from the walkabout 22
tupurlyarra	go swimming 26	waru	fire 5,7,15,18
turlku	song 2,4,20,44	warula	a fire (the -*la* ending places it as object) 18
turlkuku	for the song 4	warungka	in, on or by the fire 7,8,15
turlkukurlu	with the song 3	warungkama	by the fire 2
turlkulampa	our song 2	waruwana	around the fire 18
turlkulanyatju	give us your songs 2	watjala	tell 5,6
turlkutjanampa	their songs 4	watjarnma	telling 4
turlkuya	the songs 4	watjarnmatjana	he was telling them 3
turlpu	heart 44	watjarnu	told 4,5,6,12,15,31,36
turru	bird 44	watjarnulpira	they told him to 31
turrulu	bird did 15	watjarnulu	told her 12
tutju	girl or woman 16,17,36,44	watjarnuna	I told him 15
tuwurntjunu	pushed, buried in 8	watjarnunin	he told them 33
		watjarnuraya	they told him 22,27
wakaninpa	poking, as painting dots (originally in sand) (vi)	watjarnurni	she told me 26
Walanypa	the brolga *i.b.c.*	wayin	will it come? (conventionally used as a polite
Walanypalaltu	a lot of brolgas 33		addition to requests, the 'n' being dropped for
Walanypaya	those brolgas 33		indirect requests concerning mother-in-law) 8
Walanytja	brolgas 31,33	wayinmalpi	started crawling 24
Walanytjanga	of the brolgas 31	wayintanama	were passing by 5,35
Walanytjulu	the brolgas did 31	wayintjakutu	as he was crawling 24
Walkarli	a community 44	wilura	west 20
Walmajarri	a language group 20	wiluralu	from the west 4
walyangka	on the sand 34	wiritjana	becomes grey 26
walya	ground 44	wirlpangka	at, with or among the stars 26
Walyparnku	Black Goanna (proper name) (vi),16,18, *i.b.c.*	wirlutingu	jumped on to 5
Walyparnkulu	Black Goanna did 16	wirriyirri	wild, angry 29
Walyparnkupaltaya	they gave (dubbed) him Black Goanna 18	wirriyirringu	became angry 18
	(Yumarinyampil: Mother-in-law stealer is another	wirrtjanma	was running towards me 7
	more suggestive name)	Wirrumanu	Balgo, a place and community
walytja	own, ownership, own family, set apart (as in		(iv,v),1,43,45,53
	belonging to) 17	Wirrumanukutu	towards Wirrumanu 4
walytjakutjanampa	to her own (children, the ones) with intent 12	wirrupungulpi	she threw away 12
walytjirringka	a long time ago (implies the Dreamtime,	wirrupungulpirni	she threw it towards/on me 15
	being from the stars) 34	wirrupuwa	throw 26
wana	stick 13,44	wirrupuwalpiya	they throw (whatever it is) so that 26
wanalaya	follow 29	wirta	dog 44
wanangkuya	got their sticks 36	witulu	again (repeatedly) 8
wananma	was following 36	wiya	no 6,16,21,24,33,44
wananmaraya	they were following 24	wiyalka	oh no 8,33
wanarninpa	following 36	wiyan	not to 22

wiyangu	finished (are not, are nothing) 15	
wiyanma	finish them 5	
wiyapalara	oh no! that's not right, good 33	
wiyara	nothing for him 21	
wiyaraya	they didn't (know) 34	
wiyarna	I have nothing 6,24	
wiyarnatjananyaya	have not (have nothing) 12	
wiyarnu	finished 20	
wiyarnukatjitjanampa	when he finished it for them 4	
wiyarnungkura	I get nothing 6	
wiyarnyanamul	don't come 27	
wiyarringu	when they finished 17,22	
wiyatji	nothing 5	
wiyatju	so (degree, not condition) 7	
wiyaya	they (said) no, nothing 16	
wiyayuru	invisible 26	
wulu	kept forever 6,12,20,25,36	
wulukarra	always 36	
wulukatji	when he (kept) on 24	
wulungalta	forever, permanently 18	
wurkarlpa	green grass 5	
wurna	went 10,20,22,44	
wurnaku	to go, walk 25	
wurnarringu	ready to go 36	
wurrkaltjanu	(came) out from that grass (hiding place) 12	
wurrkulinma	feeling sorry for oneself, worrying 33	

Yaka Yaka	a place and community; Quiet-Quiet (iv,v),1,10,44,45	
yaka	quiet 34	
yakalu	quietly 12,13	
yakari	has quietened 29	
yakarn	moon 44	
yakatjunama	hiding it 7	
yakatjunamatjuran	you've been hiding (it) from me 7	
yakayanu	hidden 12	
yakayarra	hide 12	
yalkirringka	in the sky 29	
yalkirriwana	(travelling) through the sky 29	
yalurr-yalurrpa	feeling sad, sorry, grief (for someone) 21	
yanama	come 5,6,24,27,33,34	
yanamangkura	came along 27	
yanamapula	those two were going 28	
yanamara	come for him 15	
yanamaraya	they came for him 28	
yanamarniyawu	come here to me 12	
yanangkura	went away 28	
yanku	go 4,22	
yankulatjunta	we'll go to you 22	
yankun	you go 4	
yankura	going to go for him 34	
yanu	went 5,7,10,12,13,16,17,20,22,24,28,33,35	
yanulu	went to him 7,13,31,36	
yanuluya	they went to him 2	
yanupula	two went 28	
yanura	went 17	
yanutjananya	went with them 13	
yarlakulu	with a hole (refers to reed) 5	
yarltingu	called out 12	
yarltingupulampa	she sang out to them 12	
yarltingura	sang out to him 15	

yarnangungurra	the whole body 18	
yarra	go 5,6,26,29	
yarralalu	let's go to him 2	
yarrapula	gone away 10	
yarraya	all of you go 12	
yarrkala	try it 25	
yarrkanma	was trying 33	
yarrkurnu	he tried 33	
yartjiyartjimanama	made fun of him 27	
yatunma	hitting (continuously) 12	
yinira	his name 20	
yinitjunu	(they) gave him (the name) 18	
yinkalku	going to sing 4	
yinkalkuwa	to sing for us 2	
yinkarnma	was singing 4,20	
yinkarnu	sang 4,20,24	
yinkarra	singing 2	
yinkarraka	was singing in that place 2	
yinkawa	to sing (for us) 2	
yipi	mother 39,44	
yipilu	mother 26	
yirlanmatjananya	pulling them down 5	
yirna-yirna	old men 2,34	
yirnalu	the elder did 35	
yirrpintu	entered (went right through), all the way in 18	
yitiwana	alongside 5	
yiwarra	tracks 24	
yiyala	let go of 31	
yiyalkuwa	let them go, spread out, sent away 31	
yiyarnu	sent, sent away 35,36	
yulakarralu	was crying over and over 12	
yulama	crying 12,13,21,	
yulamalpi	he started crying 33	
yulanguya	cried for him 22	
yulinpa	crying 15	
yuly-yulytjarra	he kept crying 31	
yulyultjarra	evening 29	
yumari	mother-in-law, son-in-law 17,42	
Yumarinyampil	mother-in-law stealer (also black goanna, see Walyparnku)	
yumpalyarrimalpi	he was getting tired 22	
yumpalyarringurna	he became tired 24	
yumurringutjana	surrounded 28	
yungkamaraya	they were giving him 22	
yungku	give 3	
yungkurnanta	I'll give it to you 15	
yungunkutjupa-yungunkutjupa	morning after morning (yungun: tomorrow) 5	
yungunkutjupangka	next morning 2	
yunguntjarrakangku	in the morning 13	
yurlpayirra	south 20	
yurlpayirrajanu	comes from the south 34	
yurlpayirralu	from the south 4	
yurntal	daughter 39	
yurntalpa	nephews and neices 39,40,43	
yurntunma	pushing (away) 36	
yurriparni	he couldn't move 25	
yurritjunama	(they) were holding him gently 25	
yuwarrniya	give, you give (to me), say yes to me 16	
yuwayi	yes 6	
yuwu	certainly, emphatically yes 3	

The authors

Hi, my name is Gracie. I was born in 1949 at Billiluna Station. When I was older Mum and Dad took me to Balgo Mission for schooling. When I was six or seven I was put in a dormitory and was well cared for by the St John of God nuns. The Sisters taught me cooking and housekeeping during the school hours. Each week on Wednesday we also helped in the laundry. We didn't have a washing machine so we washed clothes with our hands. Now I am living at Wangkatjungka Community, Christmas Creek. I have four children, Anita sixteen, Jonathon fourteen, Vincent nine, Edith six, and we all like living here. I enjoy painting. Some of my paintings are traditional. I also like hunting, fishing and swimming.

Gracie Greene's paintings and sculptures have appeared in numerous exhibitions and publications.

Gracie, Lucille and Joe

Hi there! My name is Lucille Gill. I was born on 23rd of August 1956 at the Old Balgo mission. I speak Kukatja. I've got six brothers and three sisters. My brother Matthew Gill is an artist too. In 1986 I went to Noonkanbah with my husband. There I worked at the adult centre with Maggie Bourne the Coordinator. We did all sorts of things like making coolamons and strings of beads from seeds and hairstring. We did screen printing, lino prints and sometimes drawing. I also worked in the kindergarten at the community school. We lived at Noonkanbah for three years. We are now in Broome. I've got four children, Gloria sixteen, Harold fifteen, Maxine thirteen and Terence one year.

Paintings by Lucy Gill have appeared in several exhibitions. Her works are in private collections both in Australia and overseas including the Balance Collection of the Queensland Art Gallery.

I was born on 26th of June 1954 at Gympie, Queensland, and named Joseph Charles Allessandro Tramacchi, after my mother's favourite uncle and my grandfathers. Alessandro's father, Domenico Tramacchi, had come to Australia from Lovero, Valte Valtellina, Italy, in 1882. He worked as a charcoal burner and in the gold mines at Gympie. I'm the eldest of six children. My training as a teacher and the circumstances of living and teaching at the Jitapurru School at Wangkatjungka Community and at Kulkarriya School, Noonkanbah, have all led indirectly to my involvement with *Roughtail* and a feeling of privilege at sharing in a truly worthwhile undertaking.

Painting titles

Nyarmu

Well that's all, no more